What Others Are Saying
about R.J. Patterson

"R.J. Patterson does a fantastic job at keeping you engaged and interested. I look forward to more from this talented author."

- Aaron Patterson
bestselling author of SWEET DREAMS

DEAD SHOT

"Small town life in southern Idaho might seem quaint and idyllic to some. But when local newspaper reporter Cal Murphy begins to uncover a series of strange deaths that are linked to a sticky spider web of deception, the lid on the peaceful town is blown wide open. Told with all the energy and bravado of an old pro, first-timer R.J. Patterson hits one out of the park his first time at bat with *Dead Shot*. It's that good."

- Vincent Zandri
bestselling author of THE REMAINS

"You can tell R.J. knows what it's like to live in the newspaper world, but with *Dead Shot*, he's proven that he also can write one heck of a murder mystery."

- Josh Katzowitz
NFL writer for CBSSports.com
& author of Sid Gillman: Father of the Passing Game

"Patterson has a mean streak about a mile wide and puts his two main characters through quite a horrible ride, which makes for good reading."

- Richard D., reader

DEAD LINE

"This book kept me on the edge of my seat the whole time. I didn't really want to put it down. R.J. Patterson has hooked me. I'll be back for more."

- Bob Behler
3-time Idaho broadcaster of the year
and play-by-play voice for Boise State football

"Like a John Grisham novel, from the very start I was pulled right into the story and couldn't put the book down. It was as if I personally knew and cared about what happened to each of the main characters. Every chapter ended with so much excitement and suspense I had to continue to read until I learned how it ended, even though it kept me up until 3:00 A.M.

- Ray F., reader

DEAD IN THE WATER

"In Dead in the Water, R.J. Patterson accurately captures the action-packed saga of a what could be a real-life college football scandal. The sordid details will leave readers flipping through the pages as fast as a hurry-up offense."

- Mark Schlabach,
ESPN college sports columnist and
co-author of *Called to Coach*
and *Heisman: The Man Behind the Trophy*

THE WARREN OMISSIONS

"What can be more fascinating than a super high concept novel that reopens the conspiracy behind the JFK assassination while the threat of a global world war rests in the balance? With his new novel, *The Warren Omissions*, former journalist turned bestselling author R.J. Patterson proves he just might be the next worthy successor to Vince Flynn."

- Vincent Zandri
bestselling author of THE REMAINS

OTHER TITLES BY R.J. PATTERSON

Titus Black Thrillers
Behind Enemy Lines
Game of Shadows
Rogue Commander
Line of Fire

James Flynn Thrillers
The Warren Omissions
Imminent Threat
The Cooper Affair
Seeds of War

Brady Hawk Thrillers
First Strike
Deep Cover
Point of Impact
Full Blast
Target Zero
Fury
State of Play
Siege
Seek and Destroy
Into the Shadows
Hard Target
No Way Out
Two Minutes to Midnight
Against All Odds
Amy Means Necessary
Vengeance
Code Red
A Deadly Force
Divide and Conquer
Extreme Measures

GAME OF SHADOWS

A Titus Black novel

R.J. PATTERSON

GAME OF SHADOWS
© Copyright 2019 R.J. Patterson

First Print Edition 2020

Cover Design by Books Covered

Published in the United States of America
Green E-Books
Boise Idaho 83713

*For Bruce, a good friend
and my favorite Astros fan*

CHAPTER 1

Undisclosed Location in Russia

TITUS BLACK SCANNED the snow-dusted terrain below him through a pair of infrared binoculars. In the small farmhouse about a quarter-mile away, he identified a pair of heat signatures and plotted his next move.

"What's it looking like out there?" Christian Shields asked over the coms.

"Why don't you tell me?" Black said. "You're the one watching the entire operation unfold from that eight billion-dollar satellite."

"Fifty dollars or eight billion—nothing matters when there's thick cloud cover like there is tonight."

A flake lit on Black's nose, and he looked skyward. In an instant, he considered the new challenge facing him.

"I didn't think it was supposed to snow," he said.

"According to the forecast, it wasn't," she said.

"The chance of precipitation was only twenty percent."

"Well, they were eighty percent off," Black said, "because it's a hundred percent snowing right now."

"If you run out of ammo, at least you'll have something to hurl at the Russians."

"Cute," Black said. "Would you like for me to make a snow angel and take a picture for you?"

"I'd rather you retrieve the asset and get back to Washington so I can show you up at the range again."

Black grunted. "You know if I'd had my gun last time, you wouldn't have won."

Shields clucked her tongue. "Excuses, excuses."

The precipitation shifted from flurries to heavy snow during their conversation. The wind chilled Black's face, resulting in him tugging his bandeau scarf up around his mouth. While Black made a practice of being prepared for anything, the change in weather still surprised him. He decided he couldn't wait any longer before engaging the hostiles guarding Dr. Aaron Matthews, the American scientist who vanished without a trace two years ago.

"We'll finish this conversation after I grab Doc," Black said.

"Fair enough, but don't even think about trying to convince me to go to your range," she said.

Black huffed a soft laugh through his nose. "I

know you're scared of losing, but I promise I won't let you win every time."

"Just don't miss out there today."

"Roger that."

Black eased to his feet before crouching low and then hustling down an embankment. After moving within fifty meters of the house, he took cover behind a rusted-out tractor overrun with weeds and coated in fresh powder. As the storm grew in strength, Black recognized the window to retrieve Dr. Matthews was rapidly shrinking. But the weather wasn't the only variable outside of Black's control. The biggest one was Dr. Matthews himself.

When J.D. Blunt first briefed the Firestorm team about the assignment, a mystery remained regarding Dr. Matthews's disappearance. The FBI never definitively determined if he left on his own accord or if he was forced against his will. And while all indications pointed to abduction, Black wasn't convinced. All of Dr. Matthews's affairs were left in order as he had finalized setting up a trust fund for his college-aged daughter, Melissa, only two weeks prior to him going missing. Investigators dismissed that fact as coincidence, instead pointing to the way he left the kitchen a disaster with dishes still strewn across the stove, not to mention he had a turkey roasting in the oven. The burning smell had wafted down the hall, alerting other neighbors to the smell. When they called the building superintendent, he broke into Dr. Matthews's apartment and found the turkey charred to a crisp. Melissa had been scheduled to return home from college that weekend for Thanksgiving, but she went back earlier once authorities called her regarding her father's mysterious absence.

The FBI underwent an intensive search for a year as hundreds of people called in the hotline with tips and information regarding Dr. Matthews, but all proved to be dead ends. After the agency de-prioritized finding him, Melissa was left to dip into her trust fund to hire a private investigator to track down her father. Three days earlier, Blunt had been approached by Melissa. The PI had delivered the information but told her that he wasn't skilled enough to extract her father and needed to get someone else to finish the job. Melissa had remembered her father mentioning Blunt, mostly as a college fraternity brother but also as a Washington insider who could "get things done." So, not knowing where else to turn, she started with him. Blunt eagerly obliged.

Black peered through his binoculars one more time to check for the number of people in the building. A fire blazed inside, making it difficult to tell just how many people were in the front room. After a final assessment, he determined that there were three men inside, which meant Dr. Matthews' abduction was a certainty. Black hated being wrong, especially when after he'd ascribed nefarious motives to Dr. Matthews's disappearance. But Black couldn't help himself. General distrust for others was something he struggled to change. However, that perspective served him well as an operative, helping him avoid getting killed on several occasions. Yet this wasn't one of them.

"I'm going to engage," Black said.

"Roger that," Shields replied.

Black pulled out his rifle and steadied it on the tripod beneath the dilapidated tractor. The snow continued to increase in intensity, but it only emphasized the body heat through his scope. A minute passed before one of the men sauntered out onto the porch to smoke. With a gun draped over his shoulder, he flicked his lighter and ignited his cigarette.

With guards on the premises, Black knew they wouldn't let Dr. Matthews outside alone. They were clearly protecting the scientist from someone. Questions flooded Black's mind as he wondered who exactly Dr. Matthews needed protection from—the Americans or someone else? Perhaps there was some other group, because the U.S. intelligence community hadn't prioritized Dr. Matthews's disappearance in over a year.

After a deep breath, Black put the man in the center of the crosshairs and squeezed the trigger. He stumbled toward the railing before falling over it.

Seconds later, the other men sprang into action, setting up a bunker near the two windows flanking the front door and opening fire. Black rolled behind the tractor's back tires and waited out the barrage of bullets. For nearly a half-minute, the guards inside the house peppered the area around him, the nearby snow exploding in white puffs. When the shooting paused, Black eased his gun around one of the back wheels to survey the scene. The man who'd been shot was still lying on the ground, while two other men were preparing to shoot. However, Black began to wonder where Dr. Matthews was. The likelihood that he was fending off an attacker with the weaponry expertise the two men inside showed seemed low. Dr. Matthews didn't even own a registered weapon when he was in the U.S.

The wind continued howling, creating another misty layer of blown snow Black needed to contend with as he plotted his next move.

"Are you still flying blind out there?" Black asked over his coms.

"Pretty much," Shields said. "But I'm glad to hear your voice."

"From what I can tell, everyone in the house is firing on me. I'm not sure where the asset is."

"There might be a cellar beneath the house," she said.

"If he's even here."

"Are you starting to think this was a setup?"

"I'm not making any definitive statements at this point," Black said. "But it's certainly not out of the realm of possibility."

The firing recommenced, sending Black scurrying for cover behind the tractor again. For the next half-minute, Black withstood another round of attack. When the men started to reload, he darted to another position, reducing the angle from which he had to shoot by taking refuge behind a pile of chopped wood. The degree of difficulty required to shoot and kill the guards increased, but he would have more time to zero in on one of the hostiles while moving out of the line of fire.

Black took his time, steadied his breathing, and squeezed the trigger. He didn't wait to see if the hostile fell, instead quickly sighting in the other guard. Black fired and watched the man drop. Black switched to an assault-style weapon, opting for his Colt M4A1 over his MK11. As he moved toward the house to inspect his work, he looked at the man who'd stepped outside to smoke, the cigarette smoldering next to his hand on the blood-stained snow.

The first stair creaked as Black put pressure on it

to ease onto the porch, shattered glass from the windows crunching beneath his feet. The first guard that he shot was lying on his back, a bullet wound gaping in the man's head. Then Black spun toward the other side where he'd seen the third guard but saw nothing.

Did I miss?

The room was dark, making it difficult to see if there was any blood spattered on the floor. Black crouched to inspect, his head on a swivel. He swiped his index finger on the ground near the area where the man had fired from. Nothing but dirt. Black shined his light on the surrounding area and didn't see any apparent signs that he'd hit the man.

With him gone, Black crept from window to window around the inside of the house, peering outside with his infrared binoculars. The third man was gone.

Black muttered a long string of expletives before turning on his coms.

"Shields, has your visibility improved any?" he asked.

"It's gotten worse."

Black cursed again.

"What happened?" she asked.

"One of the hostiles is gone. I thought for sure I nailed him, but I can't find any blood."

"I know it's not the same as the range, but—"

"Save the wise cracks for later," he said. "Is there any way you can help me?"

"Unless this thick cloud cover lifts, you're on your own now."

"Roger that," Black said.

He exited through the back of the house and surveyed the area just below the steps. He knelt and studied a few imprints left behind as the snow continued to fall. After comparing one of the markings to others nearby, he determined the ones leading away from the home were much fresher.

"I've got his trail," Black said. "I'm going after him—and I'm going dark."

CHAPTER 2

Bethesda, Maryland

J.D. BLUNT WATCHED his first shot on the second hole at the Burning Tree Club skip off the fairway and over a bunker before coming to rest in the rough. He gnawed on his unlit cigar and uttered a few choice words before snatching his tee out of the ground.

NSA director, Robert Besserman, flashed a wry grin as he strode past Blunt on the way to the tee box.

"This has become a tradition," Besserman said as he gripped his club and prepared to take a shot.

"What? Me outdriving you on every hole?" Blunt said, knowing where Besserman intended to go with the snarky comment.

Besserman chuckled and didn't respond until after his strike put the ball in the center of the fairway only about ten yards shorter than where Blunt's shot landed.

"You of all people should know that it's not

about the strongest, but about who's the most precise to win these games," Besserman said.

Blunt shrugged. "I didn't account for the wind."

"I hope that's not an excuse you'd accept from one of your operatives."

"I thought you said we weren't going to talk about work today, only golf," Blunt said, a hint of sarcasm in his voice.

Besserman sighed. "Yeah, about that."

"You'd make a terrible spy, Bobby. I knew good and well something was on your mind. It's the only reason to come to this archaic club."

"No women. And no listening devices. It's the only place I ever feel comfortable playing a round of golf."

Blunt chuckled. "You do understand that your agency is why everyone is so paranoid in the first place?"

"The irony isn't lost on me, but never mind that. I couldn't risk anyone overhearing our conversation, even as unlikely as it might've been."

They both put their clubs away and climbed into the golf cart. Blunt waited until Besserman was seated before stepping on the accelerator and then navigating along the path toward their balls.

"You're starting to worry me, Bobby. You're not exactly the alarming type."

"Just consider this a warning, a friendly heads-up, if you will," Besserman said.

"What is it this time?"

"Are you aware of the newly elected freshman congressman from California? Allan Elliott?"

"Yeah, he's always on the news for the outlandish things that he says."

Besserman nodded. "That's the one."

"He's probably feeding everyone that line about how he's only doing what his constituents elected him to do."

Besserman shook his head. "Yes, publicly, that's what he's saying. But the reality is he's simply doing the bidding of Senator Wilson Wellington."

"Wellington? I should've known. Every time there's a stench on Capitol Hill, it leads right back to him."

"According to Wellington, he's a new man. And now he's out to bring about transparency to Washington."

Blunt roared with laughter. "The irony can't be lost on anyone here. He got away with murder, and now he wants to make everyone else pay? It's just absurd."

"Believe me when I say that the entire intelligence community would prefer to see him vanish from office right now. He's making things challenging for us."

"Wellington knows as well as anyone that Washington thrives in the shadows—at least when it comes to matters of national security."

"Of course he does, but all I can figure is that he wants to score political points with the younger voters in preparation for his presidential bid, even if that means pulling the covers back on even our most covert programs."

"And Firestorm is in his crosshairs?"

"Not exactly. You're safe for now. Only a couple of people on the defense committee even know if it exists. And other than a few agency heads in the know, our own intelligence community is generally unaware of what you are doing."

"But Wellington is using Elliott to stop this kind of work? How can he if he doesn't know about it?"

Besserman pointed toward his ball and gestured for Blunt to slow down. Once he stopped, the NSA director eased out and selected his club, a six iron. He smashed the ball onto the front of the green, landing about fifty feet from the pin. Once Besserman returned to the cart, he sat down and continued.

"Elliott just found out about it from Wellington. Some hacker got access to some of the committee's more specific budget approval. Don't ask me how, but there's a document floating around that lists your name on there as a consultant along with several other names and projects. And there's a hefty budget approved for that."

"Why hasn't someone stopped them?" Blunt asked.

"Several congressional members from both sides of the aisle have reached out to both Wellington and Elliott and assured them that everything in that budget is above board," Besserman said. "Even their own party has tried to put an end to this. Several of them offered Elliott seats on a couple of other prestigious committees. But that tactic backfired, making Elliott believe that there's now a better reason to continue pursuing this, especially since Wellington isn't wavering in his support of the young California congressman."

"How did he get on that committee in the first place?"

Besserman shook his head. "While he's trying to portray himself as some crusader against corruption and wasteful government spending, the report I got was that he blackmailed the committee chairman, Arnold West. And now Wellington is capitalizing on Elliott's aggressive behavior."

Blunt grunted as he applied the brakes on his cart near his ball. "Their crusade is more of a danger to our country's intelligence than anything they're going to uncover in one of those ridiculous hearings, not to mention the enormous waste of time and resources that will ultimately lead nowhere."

"At least, that's what we're hoping. Word on the street is that they intend to subpoena you since your name was listed among the consultants employed through that part of the budget. Elliott's going to ask everyone on the list about how much they make before he puts together a composite on how much money is going to clandestine operations. Once he has that number, he's going to be a royal pain in the ass. Forget the fact that he's going to put our security at risk by crippling your budget."

"Isn't there some other way around this?" Blunt asked as he stood over his ball and prepared to swing.

"At the moment, I'm afraid there isn't," Besserman said.

Blunt hit his shot true, using a four iron to drive the ball onto the center of the green, less than six feet away from the pin."

Blunt nodded toward his shot and winked at Besserman. "So when do these clowns plan to start questioning all of us?"

"Nice shot," Besserman said. "Makes up for that first one."

"It's all about how you finish."

"Touché," Besserman said. "To answer your question, Elliott has scheduled a preliminary hearing for two weeks. That should give us enough time to figure out a way to shut this down before it becomes a public relations nightmare."

"And a threat to our national security."

"That's the tack we'd like to take with this issue, but we're a little unsure about putting the squeeze on him right now since that might only make Elliott dig his heels in more."

"You just need to find the right pressure points," Blunt said. "Everybody has them."

"Don't I know that better than anybody? But if we use anything we've learned against Elliott, he could expose some of the things we're doing too—and we can't afford to have him invite the public along into a behind-the-scenes tour of how we keep our citizens safe."

"Agreed," Blunt said as he slid onto the seat behind the steering wheel and continued driving them toward the green. "But I'm sure we can come up with something else to encourage him to cooperate, maybe pressure Wellington to have Elliott drop this charade."

"Perhaps you're right, but we have to work quickly before this begins to build steam in the media. Once this hearing gets enough publicity, we're going to be stuck."

Blunt parked the cart near the green before both men got out and toted their putters toward their balls.

"Want me to hold the flag?" Blunt asked.

"Go ahead and pull it," Besserman said as he positioned himself over the ball. With a smooth stroke, the ball rolled gently downhill toward the cup, banking right before taking a sharp left turn and dropping into the hole.

Blunt's eyebrows shot upward as he prepared to make his shot. His shot circled the edge of the cup before rimming out. With an exasperated sigh, he leaned over the ball and tapped it in from six inches away.

Besserman smiled. "Like you said, J.D., it's all about how you finish."

"Double or nothing on the next hole?" Blunt asked.

"This is how you get in trouble."

"No, this is how I get out of trouble and come out a winner. Keep fighting until you emerge on top. There might be madness to my method, but there's no mystery to it."

Besserman sank into the passenger side of the cart and recorded the score for the hole. "Speaking of mysteries, there is something else I wanted to tell you about before we'll abandon all business talk for the round."

"I'm all ears," Blunt said as he climbed inside and then stomped on the gas pedal.

"It's about your operative, Titus Black."

Blunt eyed Besserman closely. "What about him?"

"It's really about his father's death."

"And?"

"There's something very strange about it. And I don't think Black got the whole truth."

"What makes you think that?" Blunt asked.

"All the records surrounding his father's final mission have been sealed. It's most curious."

"That's all you know?"

Besserman took a sip from his water bottle before continuing. "I'm just passing this along so you can look into it because I thought it might be something you'd be interested in."

"And how exactly do I do that?"

"I'd start with talking to the military judge who sealed the records, the honorable Horace Mullen."

CHAPTER 3

Undisclosed location in Russia

BLACK CREPT ALONG THE PATH marked by the fleeing hostile's footprints in the snow. The driving wind wasn't helpful, but Black looked on both sides of an ever-growing bank outlining a trail into the thick woods. While the close inspection of the markings slowed his speed, he couldn't afford to lose the one man still alive who might be the lead to Dr. Matthews.

According to the dossier Black received, Dr. Matthews earned a PhD from Stanford University in Mechanical Engineering, focusing on ultrasonic research. He later became a tenured professor at MIT before he began consulting with the U.S. military. However, his top-secret work was in its infancy when he vanished two years ago. And while there was no proof that the Russians had nabbed Dr. Matthews, all signs pointed to them as the ones responsible for the doctor's abduction. Yet after a year of searching, the intelligence community failed to find even the slightest suggestion that Dr. Matthews was in the Russians' custody. As the night wore on, Black was beyond convinced that he had been wrong to assume Dr. Matthews disappeared on purpose and the FBI was wrong to ever stop looking for him. If he wasn't such a prized commodity, the Russians wouldn't have three agents protecting him.

But where was Dr. Matthews?

The one man who might know was still lurking in the thick brush somewhere nearby. And Black needed to find the Russian agent before he disappeared too.

Black stopped as he noticed the tracks veered off the path and ventured farther into the woods. He knelt down to inspect them more closely. After removing his pack, he dug inside and fished out his night vision goggles. Once he situated them and turned them on, he entered the surrounding forest.

Branches hung low, straining to sustain the burden of the thickening snow. The wind continued to whip through the trees, sending occasional parcels of snow and ice crashing to the ground. After maneuvering toward a fallen pine, he crouched down and scanned the area. The exercise seemed futile as he slowly peered through the vegetation, unable to identify anything out of place. But after his third sweeping look at the area, he saw a glimmer of heat.

At first, Black wondered if he'd just seen a rabbit bounding along in search of a late-night snack. Black glued his gaze to the spot and waited. After about a minute, he saw slight movement again, but not the kind an animal would make. The bushes moved and Black clearly saw the outline of a person.

Black mentally marked the location before easing east in an attempt to circle behind the man for a surprise attack. Methodically, Black moved well outside of the hostile's direct line of sight. The entire journey took at least ten minutes, but the man remained in the same position, either unwilling or unable to move.

Just as Black slipped into position to pounce, the man stood. He was heavily armed with one gun in his hands and two others draped over his back. Black retreated behind the closest tree and watched as the guard looked to his left and then right, acting as if he heard something. Black snatched a pinecone off a low-hanging branch and hurled it to the man's right. He glanced in that direction, creating all the opportunity Black needed.

He approached the man from his blind spot on the left and leaped onto his back. His knees buckled beneath Black's weight as the two men tumbled to the ground. While the Russian tried to free himself, Black used his knee to pin down the man's right hand.

"Gde on?" Black said in German. " Where is he?"

"Who?"

"Don't play dumb with me," Black said as he secured the man's other hand behind his back and used a zip tie to bind them together. "Where is Dr. Matthews?"

"I don't know who you are talking about," the Russian said.

His sincerity was difficult to question given the quiver in his voice.

"I'm only going to ask you once more," Black said. "Where is Dr. Matthews?"

The man struggled to turn over, but he couldn't. Unable to break Black's grip, the man simply turned his head and spat at Black.

"Go to hell," the man said.

"It doesn't have to end this way," Black said. "It's simple. You give me a location, and I let you go free."

"I don't know what you're talking about."

"Who hired you?" Black asked with a growl.

The man set his jaw, refusing to answer.

"Is this really worth dying over?" Black asked as he tightened his grip. "That is the question you have to answer for yourself."

"Probably not," the man said before he made

one final attempt to escape Black. When the Russian turned, he managed to get Black off balance for a moment. That was all the man needed to spin free and turn the tables. With his wrists still bound together, he threw his hands over a stunned Black from behind, placing him in a chokehold. The Russian pulled hard against Black's throat, forcing him to gasp for air and drop his weapon. In an attempt to regain control, Black leaned forward, forcing the man off the ground. Black staggered backward and slammed the hostile against a tree. Once his grip loosened, Black ducked out of the hold and spun around. He snatched his gun off the ground and put three bullets in the man, two in his center mass and the final one in his head.

Black turned his coms back on. "I'm done here."

"No sign of Dr. Matthews?" Shields asked.

"Unfortunately not," he said as he pillaged the man's pockets. "This felt like a setup."

"So do you still think Dr. Matthews went willingly?"

Black placed his hand on something inside of the man's pockets. "Hard to say. I wish he was here to answer that question for himself."

Black dug out a matchbook and studied it before flipping it open. The logo for the Savoy Hotel was emblazoned on the outside, but the note scrawled on the inside made his eyes widen.

"I certainly didn't expect that," Black said after a brief pause.

"What is it?" she asked.

"I found a matchbook from the Savoy Hotel in Zurich, and there's a message in it."

"What's it say?"

"J.D. Blunt, come and find me—Antoine."

CHAPTER 4

Beaufort, S.C.

BLUNT LUMBERED ALONG THE DOCK that hung out over the murky waters of Brickyard Creek. The late autumn weather was on full display in the nation's capital with Thanksgiving drawing near, but in the South Carolina low country, only a slight reduction in the humidity hinted that it wasn't still summertime. While mopping his brow with a handkerchief, Blunt stopped to survey the calm waters drifting along. And for a moment, he wished he was the one waxing his boat like Horace Mullen was instead of paying the judge a visit in what promised to be a contentious conversation.

"Judge Mullen?" Blunt called as he resumed his walk along the weathered wooden planks.

Mullen was polishing the outside of the boat with a rag when he looked up. His mouth fell agape as he climbed onto the dock.

"As I live and breathe," he said. "If it isn't J.D. Blunt?"

Blunt forced a smile and offered his hand. "I'm still living and breathing, which is a good thing."

"Damn right it is," Mullen said. "It's been, what, fifteen years since I last saw you?"

Blunt shrugged. "Beats me. All I know is that it's been a while."

"Well, let's go to the porch and have a beer," Mullen said, starting toward the house. "It's been far too long. We need to catch up."

"I'm afraid this isn't that kind of visit."

Mullen stopped and turned around, scowling as he did. "What's this about? It's not my grandson, is it? Did something happen to him at West Point?"

"As far as I know, everything with him is fine," Blunt said. "You don't think the government hired me to deliver news of service deaths to family members, do you?"

"Well, I didn't know what to think when you came charging onto my property like this. I assume you're either to tell me really bad news or you just wanted to check in on how an old friend is doing."

"I have a phone for that," Blunt said. "But maybe we should go up to the porch and have a drink. This might take a while."

"I'm expecting a buddy to come over shortly, so

it can't take that long—unless of course you'd like to come with us. Three rods in the water are always better than two."

Blunt shook his head. "I wish I could join you, but maybe another time, okay?"

"Fine, but now you're starting to make me nervous," Mullen said. "One of those killers I locked up isn't on the loose, is he?"

Blunt pointed toward the house. "Let's just go have a seat, and I'll tell you all about it."

Mullen led his unexpected guest onto the porch and then offered him a chair. Blunt took a deep breath and then drank in the view. Disappearing to a place like Mullen's wouldn't be so bad. Fishing most days, reclining in a hammock and reading a good Tom Clancy novel on others—that was a rhythm Blunt could appreciate. But that dream was still far off. He cared too much about his country to do nothing while either terrorists or corrupt political leaders destroyed it.

And the latter was exactly why he was paying Mullen a visit.

"You still drink bourbon?" Mullen asked as he sauntered over to his small bar on the edge of his porch.

Blunt sighed. "That question never needs to be asked."

Mullen laughed and poured a pair of drinks. He handed one of them to Blunt as they settled into their chairs.

"So what's this all about, J.D.? You're acting a little cagier than normal."

"We've known each other for a long time, right?"

Mullen nodded. "At least forty years."

"And you wouldn't lie to me, would you?"

"Of course not. That's absurd. I know I can shoot you straight about everything."

Blunt eyed Mullen closely. "Everything?"

"Just say it, J.D. I don't have time for games."

Blunt took a long pull on his drink before setting it down on the railing and then leaning forward in his seat. "It's very important that you're completely honest with me because I'm in the midst of trying to flush out some unsavory characters in Washington—and I don't want you to go down with them."

"Wha—what are you talking about? You know I've never been anything but above board with you, not to mention all my dealings from the bench."

"That's why I'm here, to verify that. Because there's some shady stuff going on and I need your help to find out what the truth is."

Mullen held out his hands. "Just ask the damn question. You don't need to preface anything with me."

Blunt shrugged. "Okay, here it goes. There was a Capt. Black who was downed in action during the war in Afghanistan. His body was supposedly dragged through the streets by Taliban soldiers. However, you sealed his records—and I want to know why."

"Come on, J.D. You expect me to remember something like that?"

"Not only do I expect you to remember it, I expect you to tell me why. You were a military judge, and concealing a full report from a deceased soldier's family isn't exactly an everyday occurrence."

"That's where you're wrong. I sealed plenty of files, mostly as a security measure. If some of those files ever became public, an immeasurable amount of damage could be done."

Blunt narrowed his eyes. "You know damn well that's not always the case. It's certainly not the case here. So, are you going to play nice here or not?"

"J.D., you know I like you. I'm telling you that I don't remember that specific case."

"And I'm telling you that I don't believe you. Right now, you must choose if you're going to help me out or stand in my way. And I think you know how I feel about people who stand in my way."

Mullen exhaled and stared off in the distance. "Look, I didn't really have a choice."

"Oh, come on. I don't have the time or the

patience to listen to your excuses."

"You don't want to meddle in this. Trust me."

Blunt glared at Mullen. "Meddle? You think uncovering the truth is meddling? What happened to you?"

"There are times when it's just better to not ask questions. This is one of those times."

"That's not something I do."

Mullen shook his head. "If you knew what was good for you, you would. And I'm willing to forget this entire conversation ever took place if you just ask me about how Darla is doing or the kids."

"Darla has a husband. Your kids have a father. But Capt. Black's family and friends don't have that luxury. They're just left to twist in the wind, thanks to you. No answers. No real closure. Just some manufactured tale designed to protect the corruption leeching through military command in the desert."

"You've got it all wrong, J.D."

"Do I? It's up to you to prove otherwise."

Mullen pointed at Blunt. "I know what you're trying to do here. It's not going to work. You can pretend like everything is black and white, but it's not."

Blunt threw back his glass, draining the last drop of bourbon. He slammed the tumbler on the railing and stood.

"So this is how it has to be?" Mullen asked.

"No, it isn't. But this is how you're choosing to make it. May God have mercy on your soul."

Blunt didn't turn around as he marched down the steps and around the house, ignoring the calls of Mullen.

"You're going to regret this," Mullen shouted.

Blunt waved his hand dismissively, refusing to turn around.

No, you're going to regret it. And you'll spend the rest of your life doing so.

That much Blunt was going to make sure of.

CHAPTER 5

Zurich, Switzerland

BLACK SMOOTHED HIS mustache along his upper lip as he strode through the doors of the Savoy Hotel, twirling his cane. Before he left for the appointment, he joked with Shields that he should have a top hat as well to complete the look. He rubbed his eyes, itching from the contacts that turned his irises green instead of his natural crystal blue that usually sparkled in the light.

"How's Charlie Chaplin doing today?" Shields asked over the coms.

"You think you're funny, don't you? This is all your suggestion, so you better not mock it."

"It looked far less conspicuous in my head."

"Great," Black said and then sighed. "You think my cover is going to be blown within a few seconds of entering the room with Antoine?"

"Only if you pull out your guns and shoot him,"

Shields said. "This is sheerly for my pleasure."

"I gathered as much. Well, I hope you're getting your money's worth because I'll never do this again."

"Now where have I heard that before?" Shields asked.

"Here's a little pro tip for you: stop while you're ahead."

Shields chuckled. "Oh, I don't just intend to get ahead in this little gambit. I fully intend to win by crushing your soul."

"One day you're going to regret how heartless you are."

"Until that day comes, I'm going to enjoy every minute of your misery as a Charlie Chaplin double."

"I hate you."

Black strode up to the concierge desk, hooking the nook of his cane on the edge of the counter. Ever since his showdown in Russia with the assassin, Shields launched into a furious investigation as to who Antoine was and why he'd left a brazen note for J.D. Blunt on the dead assassin. And her findings on the dark web gave her the protocol for connecting with the mastermind behind the plot to capture Blunt's attention. According to Shields's discovery, Black needed to ask for Antoine at the concierge desk between 2:30 and 3:00 p.m. with a specific catchphrase.

The young man sitting at the concierge station was swiping at his phone but looked up quickly when Black spoke.

"Do you believe impossible things?" Black asked the man.

He paused for a moment before responding. "I prefer the ones that are curiouser and curiouser."

"We're all mad here, aren't we?"

The concierge flashed a faint grin. "Indeed we are. Need directions to the rabbit hole?"

"I thought you'd never ask."

The man opened up the bottom desk drawer and dug out a small notepad. He scribbled down a number on a piece of paper and folded it up before handing it to Black.

"Thank you," Black said.

"Be there at 3:30, not a minute before or after."

"I understand," Black said before he snatched his cane and turned to walk away.

"You must be precise," the young man said again.

Black nodded without turning around. He hooked the crook of his cane over his forearm and continued across the lobby. Once he reached the street, he turned on his coms.

"You there?" Black asked.

"That didn't take long," Shields said. "Did you get the contact information?"

"Of course. You never cease to amaze me."

She chuckled. "You're making me blush."

"I doubt that."

"Of course you aren't. But you know how much I love to hear you heap praise in my direction."

"Well, you deserve it," Black said. "That was about as easy as it gets, and it was all thanks to you."

"Thank me later, after we catch this bastard," she said. "We still have plenty of work to do before we figure out who Antoine is and why he's trying to bait Blunt into meeting with him."

"We'll figure that out soon enough," Black said.

"Just be careful. Whoever this guy is, he's dangerous."

"And he's going to pay for his little stunt."

"Can you do me a favor this time?"

"What's that?"

"Just don't hurt him until you get some information out of him," she said.

"The guy in Russia was trying to kill me. I didn't have a choice."

"Sure, but this is different," she said. "He'll be expecting you, and we have no idea what he's after."

"You still confident Blunt isn't going to go ballistic when he learns that we left him out of the loop?"

Shields sighed. "Look, it's better that he didn't

know until we understand what's going and who it is we're up against. And at the end of the day, he's going to be more upset that we didn't come back with Dr. Matthews than anything else—unless we can deliver on this."

"I don't care if Blunt's mad at me," Black said. "He's been angry at me plenty of times before—and I doubt I'll forever avoid his wrath in the future. Getting the job done is what he cares about the most. And that's something we didn't do."

"Not yet, anyway. But there's still plenty of time to make up for that."

"If Dr. Matthews is even alive," Black said.

"And if he is, I'm sure we'll bring him home safely."

"Roger that."

Black entered a coffee shop across the street and ordered a mocha, killing time until his appointment with the mysterious Antoine.

At five minutes before the scheduled time, Black headed back to the hotel and to the designated room. He stood outside and waited until the long hand swept onto the six. Forming a fist to knock, Black never made contact with the door before it swung open.

Filling up the frame was a hulking man, casting a shadow that extended into the hallway. At six foot four, Black rarely found himself looking up at someone. Two inches taller than Black, the man appeared as if he lived in a gym. The man's muscles bulged through his shirt, so tight that it looked like it was painted on.

"Welcome to The Mad Hatter," the man said in a clipped-Russian accent before gesturing for Black to enter.

Black stepped inside and examined the room. "I thought this was a hotel room."

"It is," the man said as he patted Black down for weapons. "But I conduct my business out of here on occasion, weapon free of course."

The room was stripped of any furniture and decor that would suggest the space was normally rented out to guests. The walls were painted a solid maroon, interrupted only by a dark wooden arm rail. In a small sitting area, Black saw two white couches, simple in their modern design and stark in their contrast to the dark hues elsewhere. A wooden coffee table was positioned between the two sofas and contained a tray with a steel teapot and two porcelain cups with saucers.

"Join me," the man said, nodding toward the couch.

Black eased into the seat and eyed the man carefully. "Are you Antoine?"

"Would you stay if I wasn't?" the man asked before he clipped the end of a cigar and ignited it with a butane lighter.

Black shrugged and watched the man blow a thick ring of smoke into the air.

"That's not an answer," the man said.

"There are other ways to communicate besides words," Black said. "I've found that sometimes talking is a waste of breath."

"You're a man of action, aren't you, Mr. Black?"

"Excuse me?" Black asked, furrowing his brow and cocking his head to one side.

"You're disguise might fool most people, but I know who you are. And I know why you're here."

"Perhaps my disguise isn't for you," Black said.

The man's eyes lit up as he leaned forward. "So you are Mr. Black?"

"Well, I'm not Mrs. Black. But I'm also not here to sip tea and discuss our latest favorite quiche recipes."

"In that case, my question is this: Why are you even here at all?"

Black smoothed his mustache and glanced up at the ceiling before responding. "If you know so much about me, you tell me why I'm here."

The man stood and cracked his knuckles. "I guess since you're about to die, I could give you the common courtesy of telling you who's going to kill you and why."

"Let's hear it," Black said.

"My name is Antoine," the man said. "And I used to do favors for your boss, J.D. Blunt. That's why I summoned him."

"And you knew he wouldn't come."

Antoine shrugged. "Does he even know you're here?"

"What difference does it make?"

"Perhaps I'll leave a message in your pocket if he's not aware of what you're doing."

"You do what you feel is best, if you manage to survive yourself."

Antoine grinned wryly. "Ah, a fellow believer in the principle of mutually assured destruction. It's really a shame that I'm going to have to kill you. We could've gotten along famously."

"Perhaps I wasn't clear," Black said. "I have every intention of walking out that door. And it's gonna take more than you to stop me."

Antoine laughed and shook his head. "You have all the bravado of a Blunt hire."

"You're also going to find out just how much bravado in a moment when I start wailing on your face."

"You're also very loyal, which I must warn you is a mistake," Antoine said. "Blunt isn't who he says he is. He's got a dark side, one that nobody knows about. He acts as if he's the one who's been appointed to maintain the moral compass of humanity. But the truth is far from that. He's just like everyone else, manipulating the system for his personal gain."

"Now I know you're a liar."

"Have you ever stopped to ask yourself how many safe houses he really needs? Are those houses he purchased with a government budget or ones he took for himself by skimming something off the top? I would tell you to go look up the deeds, but you're not going to get the chance. So, I'll tell you myself. He owns a company that serves as a shell for all his illegal business activities—Blue Moon Rising Enterprises LLC."

"I've heard enough," Black said. "I get it. You don't like him. But I'm done listening to your drivel."

Without another word, Black lunged toward the man and drove him backward into the couch. Black tightened his grip as they tumbled across the floor. He delivered two close-body punches before Antoine could strike back. But when he did, he smashed his fist into Black's jaw and then kicked him against the wall.

Stunned by the blow and aching from the pain of the hit, Black grunted as he scrambled to his feet, just in time to brace for another blow from a charging attack. Antoine drove his shoulder into Black's stomach and pinned him against the wall. But Black pushed back and slammed his knee into Antoine's face. With Antoine reeling for the first time since the fight began, Black didn't waste the opportunity to seize the upper hand and pursued his retreating host. Antoine staggered backward, trying to recover from the flurry of blows. The wall stopped him, allowing him to regain his balance. As he did, he hiked up his pants leg and retrieved a knife.

Black was about to barrel into Antoine when the blade came out. While Black wanted more answers— particularly who Antoine was and what was his real beef with Blunt—surviving to fight again ruled his quick decision-making process. Black spun toward the exit, leaping over a couch and racing into the hallway. He hustled down the large open staircase that was encircled by all the rooms on each floor.

Antoine ran after Black but stopped at the landing. "That's right. Run, you coward."

Black passed a couple of slack-jawed guests on the steps, refusing to look back at Antoine.

"Shields, do you copy?" Black asked.

"Loud and clear," she said. "Do you need any assistance?"

"Yeah, but not the kind you might think I'd want right now."

"Then tell me what you need."

Black maneuvered around a bellhop guiding a

luggage cart toward the elevator before putting a shoulder into the front door to fling it open. He took a deep breath and surveyed his surroundings before glancing back up at the third floor balcony where Antoine stood, leaning with both hands on the railing. He nodded subtly at Black.

"I need you to find out what Antoine was talking about," he said.

"Regarding what exactly?"

"Regarding Blunt."

CHAPTER 6

Washington, D.C.

BLUNT WALKED UP TO the security checkpoint outside the White House and handed his credentials to the guard. He winked at Blunt before scanning the access badge. Two weeks after Michaels's election, the president set up a monthly meeting with Blunt in an advisory role on issues of national security. While Blunt didn't always have much to offer, he relished the opportunity to influence the nation's leader.

"Looks like everything is in order, Senator Blunt," the guard said as he handed the access badge back to Blunt.

"Please, just call me J.D., Clarence," Blunt said. "We've been doing this long enough that we should both be on a first name basis."

"You know I can't do that, Senator," Clarence said with a smile, "but it's mighty nice of you to offer every month. Enjoy your visit at the White House."

Blunt shrugged. "You know I'm going to ask you to call me by my first name the next time I see you, don't you?"

Clarence smiled and nodded. "Yes, sir. I'd be surprised if you didn't."

"Tell Louise hello for me," Blunt said. "And Christmas is just around the corner. I'm still hoping for more of the frosted sugar cookies she always makes."

"Of course, sir. I'm sure she'll be baking up a batch soon enough. I'll save you one."

Blunt smiled and waved before he draped the lanyard with his access badge around his neck. He continued to the staff entrance for the White House and was greeted solemnly by a pair of Secret Service agents who screened his briefcase and then walked him through a metal detector.

Once they waved him through, Blunt went to his assigned location to connect with Michaels. Keeping their visits out of the whispers of the administration's gossip mill was important to the president. While their meetings were above board, Michaels expressed numerous times that he preferred to shield his policy influencers from any public outcry that might result if knowledge of their conversations became public.

Blunt entered the passcode on the access pad, and the door unlocked with a click. He went inside and secured the door behind him before taking a seat on the couch against the far wall in the cramped, stark room. One small coffee table and a pair of sitting chairs were the only furnishings. While he waited for the president, he dug out a file folder and placed it in the center of the table.

After five minutes, Michaels slipped inside the room.

"Sorry to keep you waiting," Michaels said.

Blunt smiled as he stood, offering his hand. "No worries. I just took the time to lay out some of the reports I wanted to show you regarding what we discovered in the aftermath of that attack last month at the Kennedy Center."

Michaels waved off Blunt. "I'm not interested in any of that today."

"You're not?" Blunt said as he furrowed his brow. "You had a front-row seat to a near assassination of the Ukranian president. Aren't you the least bit curious about how that plot came to be?"

"Honestly, no. We already know that the traitor who was involved in that coup is now dead. Titus Black won't be bothering us ever again."

"I'm afraid we may have jumped to conclusions about that, and I—"

Michaels waved dismissively. "What does it matter? I'm safe. The Ukranian president is still alive.

And Titus Black is dead."

"But, sir, I—"

"Look, J.D., I keep you involved with national security because of your expertise in shedding light on what lurks in the shadows. I don't need you to go on some vigilante crusades."

Blunt scowled. "Vigilante crusades? I'm not sure how digging deeper into this conspiracy constitutes a vigilante crusade."

"I'm not talking about this," Michaels said, gesturing toward the papers on the coffee table. "I'm referring to the little visit you recently paid Horace Mullen."

"How did you know that?"

"Horace called me and told me that you were snooping around about some military ruling he made to seal records years ago," Michaels said.

"There's more to it than that. I was just—"

"I don't care what your reasons are or what you think you might know about that case, just drop it."

"If there's something worth investigating, I'll look into it. How can I give you sound advice about anything without looking further into a situation like this? I need to make sure everything I'm telling you has been vetted several times over before I bring it to you."

"Trust me when I say this: You're better off

leaving this one alone."

"Is there something you're not telling me, sir?"

"J.D., I forget more secrets in a day than I can count. That's just how it is when you reach the executive branch of the government. I'm here to govern and do so off sound information from trust sources like you. I can't have you running around trying to look into a twenty-year-old case that literally has no bearing on national security."

"So you are familiar with what happened to Capt. Black?"

Michaels nodded. "And it doesn't matter. He's gone."

"What about justice for those he's left behind?"

"Most of them are dead, including his son. Why don't you just let a sleeping dog lie?"

Blunt eased back in his seat. "Look, I don't want to stick my nose where it doesn't belong and—"

"Good," Michaels said. "I'm glad that's settled. If you only knew what it was like for just a day to walk in my shoes, you'd know that there are plenty of stories that are best left buried for the sake of everyone involved."

"Just shoot me straight on this issue: Was Capt. Black's mission sabotaged?"

Michaels bit his lip and slowly shook his head. "Of course not. Now, let's move on, shall we?"

Blunt nodded and dug out another set of documents from his briefcase before sliding it toward Michaels. "I thought you might want to have a look at these."

Michaels's eyebrows shot upward as he perused the page. "Have you verified all of this?"

Blunt nodded. "I spoke with an agent last week who has demonstration footage of the weapon."

"I'd like to see that—and then get it to the Security Council. We need to make sure nobody else gets their hands on this."

Blunt nodded. "Of course, sir."

He collected all the documents and stood before offering his hand. Michaels shook it and then slapped Blunt on the back.

"I appreciate all you do, J.D.," Michaels said. "I'm not sure my administration could make the best decisions if not for your wisdom."

"Thank you, sir," Blunt said.

Michaels exited the room, and Blunt followed protocol, waiting five minutes before leaving. And he spent all five of those minutes stewing over Michaels's response.

Blunt, like any good poker player, excelled when it came to picking up someone else's tell. Michaels's was slight, barely noticeable to most people. But to Blunt, Michaels's tick might was well have been a flashing red light accompanied by a siren: Whenever Michaels bit his lip, he was lying.

Like hell I'm gonna let a sleeping dog lie.

Blunt left the White House more determined than ever to find out what exactly Judge Mullen and Michaels were intent on hiding. Even though Blunt had to leave in the morning for a short trip to Geneva, he wasn't about to delay his hunt for the truth about what really happened to Capt. Black in Afghanistan.

CHAPTER 7

Tangiers, Morocco

BLACK AND SHIELD AWAITED Blunt at the Firestorm safe house overlooking the Mediterranean. A cool breeze wafted across the veranda, chilling Black as he scanned the water below. While he longed to simply drink in the serene vista where sailboats dotted the seascape, he couldn't help himself. He studied each vessel, attempting to determine if anyone of them could be spying on the Firestorm team's conversation.

Shields sauntered up to next to him and then rested on her elbows atop the waist-high stone wall. "Are you thinking what I'm thinking?"

"Only if you have a hunch that the blue sailboat down there is being manned by a pair of Russian SVR agents," Black said, his eyes still fixed on the horizon.

"And this is why you belong in the field permanently."

Black shrugged. "Maybe it'd do me some good

to sit still in a chair for a few weeks. It might tamp down all this paranoia I have."

"That's what makes you a great agent," Blunt said, his voice arresting their attention.

Black and Shields turned around to find their director wearing a gray suit and a wide grin.

"Come, let's go inside where we can have a conversation free of any prying ears," Blunt said, gesturing them toward the door. "The blue sailboat is definitely two operatives trying to eavesdrop on us."

"I knew it," Black said as he followed Shields and Blunt inside.

Blunt shook his head. "If you couldn't pick them out, I would seriously consider re-assigning you to some position more suitable for your poor observational skills."

"We could stay out on the porch and give them some bad information," Shields suggested.

"Not today," Blunt said. "We don't need to misdirect them, especially since we don't even know if they're here for us."

"Who else could they be here for?" she asked.

"Take your pick—MI6 has a safe house two doors down, as do the Chinese. It's a neighborhood of spies."

"And you know this how?" she asked.

"Because one intelligence group I consulted with

built this entire enclave of houses and targeted foreign agencies as buyers," Blunt said. "And let's just say that it's turned into a gold mine of information for us."

"Slick," Shields said. "I wouldn't have thought of that."

"Don't worry," Blunt said. "I have some friends who've vetted every seller and builder of the homes where you both live. You can never be too sure."

They all sat down in the living room in front of the cozy fire Black had started earlier.

"I think we'd both agree with that sentiment after what just happened in Zurich," Black said.

Blunt fished a cigar out of his pocket and clipped the end. He commenced to chewing on the stogie, staring off with a pensive look before turning his gaze toward his two agents.

"You said it was urgent that we speak," Blunt said. "That's why I delayed my trip to Geneva for a day."

"And we appreciate that," Shields said. "We didn't really feel like this was the sort of thing that could wait."

"That bad, huh?" Blunt asked.

"Bad would be an understatement," Black said. "There's someone actively hunting you, and this someone doesn't just want to chat."

"He's hostile?"

"I bet he'd disembowel you if given the opportunity," Black said. "He has a serious vendetta against you. To be quite frank, I'm not sure it's safe for you to be in Switzerland right now. If he knew you were there and walking around in the open, he might come after you."

"I'm not even leaving the airport," Blunt said. "It's just a quick exchange there and I'll be back in Washington by tomorrow afternoon."

"What kind of exchange?" Shields asked.

"That information is need-to-know," Blunt said. "Now, what else did you learn in your interaction with Antoine?"

"Well, not much," Black said. "He seemed somewhat obsessed with you."

"So, you don't know anything about Dr. Matthews?"

Black shook his head. "The whole thing felt like a setup, like he knew you would send an agent—and that your agent would likely prevail against the men he hired. Perhaps he just wanted to lure you to the Savoy Hotel where he could kill you."

Blunt pulled the cigar out of his mouth and grunted. "Antoine had to know I would never walk into a situation like that. He's a sharp agent."

"Think he just wanted to kill one of your agents to prove a point?" Shields asked.

Blunt pointed at her and nodded. "Now, that's the most likely scenario. He's still very bitter."

Black learned forward in his chair. "About what?"

Blunt stood up and sauntered over to the wet bar in the corner of the room. He poured himself a drink and then paced around.

"Several years ago, Antoine wanted to work for me. He was a Russian operative who had a bounty placed on his head by the SVR. The Russians were convinced he was a spy. To our knowledge, he wasn't. But someone had framed him. So, instead of pleading his case to his own government, he offered his valuable knowledge and services to the U.S. in exchange for asylum and protection."

"Yet he hates you?" Shields asked. "There must be more to this story."

"I can't go into all the details, but Antoine auditioned to be an agent for me," Blunt said.

Black got up and fixed a drink for Shields and himself. He handed one to her and then sat back down. "Apparently, that didn't work out as he'd hoped."

"Or me either," Blunt said. "My expectations were that he'd be able to infiltrate certain illegal arms markets for us and give us some insight into what the trends were among terrorists in the Middle East and figure out what opportunities we might have to infiltrate some of those tight circles, basically anything to give us an edge in snuffing out attacks before they happen."

"I take it he didn't pass his assignment," Shields suggested.

"Quite the contrary," Blunt said. "He passed it with flying colors. I had him take out a Chinese assassin, Wei Ying, we'd been struggling to eliminate for years. He'd made a name for himself by throwing people off tall buildings, deaths that were all classified as suicides."

"I think I remember a rash of men from the financial sector leaping to their deaths in China a few years back," Shields said.

"Nobody was jumping off roofs," Blunt said. "Those men were all successful and hadn't acquiesced to the demands of the Chinese government, which proved to be their ultimate downfall, no pun intended."

"So you had Antoine eliminate Ying?" Black asked.

Blunt took a long pull on his drink. "It was a day that intelligence agents the world over celebrated. By our best guess, Ying had killed more than four dozen operatives affiliated with various governments the world over. I know he'd taken out more than a dozen of the CIA's men and women."

"He seems exactly like the kind of guy you're looking for," Black said.

Blunt shrugged. "If he were, you wouldn't be sitting here right now. I gave the position to you."

Black's eyes widened. "So I was your second choice?"

"You were my first," Blunt said. "The two of you were evenly matched skill wise, but I didn't fully trust him for some reason. Maybe it's only because he wanted the position due to the SVR targeting him for elimination; I don't know. But at the end of the day, I just didn't feel right about it. Something in my gut told me to do otherwise. I can't really explain it."

Black sighed. "Well, now he's ready to make you pay."

"It won't be any time soon since he's on dozens of blacklists and wanted by Interpol for some other crimes he's since committed," Blunt said. "There's no way he could even get into the U.S. right now. But when he decides to make a run at me, I'll be ready."

"Will you?" Black asked.

"Without a doubt."

Blunt's phone rang, so he excused himself from the room. Black and Shields discussed the conversation that had just occurred.

"Are you thinking what I'm thinking?" Shields asked.

"Only if you're thinking about devouring some lamb roast tonight at that tavern downtown where we ate last time," he said as he sat back down.

"You know what I'm talking about."

Black took a deep breath. "I don't know. As you well know, my trust is always in short supply. But if I had to give to anyone, Blunt would get the benefit of the doubt."

"Why do I get the sense that you're trying to convince yourself of this fact?"

"Maybe because we both get the sense that Blunt is hiding something," Black said.

Moments later, Blunt returned to the room, tapping his cell phone against the palm of his left hand. "Looks like you don't need to worry about my trip to Switzerland after all."

Black sat upright in his chair. "Why's that?"

"That was Besserman," Blunt said. "We just got a hit on Antoine. He's in Merano, Italy."

"That still doesn't solve the problem of where Dr. Matthews is, or if this is even about him," Shields said.

"Which is why you two are going to Merano tonight to find out what's really going on," Blunt said. "And good luck, you two."

CHAPTER 8

THE WINDSHIELD WIPERS swung furiously back and forth as Black navigated the SUV up the twisting mountain road. All of the surrounding peaks were heavily coated as most of the ski resorts in the picturesque Alps had opened early thanks to record amounts of snowfall. Black leaned forward and nodded toward the mansion overhanging the valley.

"There it is," he said to Shields. "The home of Salvatore Duca, the boss of the Mala del Brenta mafia operation."

"I thought that group disappeared a long time ago," she said.

"They did. And Duca wisely relocated up here out of the public eye, building a veritable fortress. He took over the assets after the last boss died, doled them out to many of the members, and then announced that they were closed for business."

Shields chuckled. "And people bought that?"

"I guess if you lay low long enough, people will forget about you," Black said. "The latest briefing on Duca I read said that he was partnering with another crime family, working as a subsidiary, if you will. Pretty smart, if you ask me."

"He must line some politicians' pockets to get away with the ruse that he isn't involved in organized crime anymore."

"Of course," Black said, nodding in agreement. "This is Italy, the birthplace of corruption in the west. Of all the great things Rome gave us, greedy politicians and corrupt leadership ranks at the top of the list."

"And the rest of the world has seen that as some blueprint instead of a cautionary tale."

"If they didn't, we might have to do some boring job," Black said. "Maybe you'd be a tax accountant."

"I'm sure I'd find something slightly more interesting than that."

"Wouldn't take much, would it?" Black said with a wink.

He continued along the road, which overlooked the Passer River flowing down the mountain, which was still flowing steadily. They drove along in silence for a few minutes until they drew closer to the gate leading up to Duca's property.

Both sporting catering attire, they stopped a few hundred meters shy of the estate, just around a bend that wasn't visible from the front entrance. Black popped the hood and got out. He put a white flare on the engine block and waited for the next guest to approach.

"I really hope this works," Shields said. "I'm not too keen on getting buried at the bottom of this valley."

Black chuckled. "You think these guys are going to bury us if they catch us? We'll be chopped up into tiny little pieces and fed to their dogs."

"You have such a way with imagery," she said. "I think I'm going to throw up now."

"Not yet. You have to save that as part of your fake pregnancy shtick if we can't get anyone to buy that we're really part of the catering crew."

"We only have one shot," she said. "If you're having doubts about which plan is going to work, we should switch now."

Black pursed his lips as he stared down the road at a pair of headlights heading toward them. "No, this is the ticket. Duca's daughter is turning eighteen tonight. They will want every person on hand to help with the massive amount of guests."

"How many did you say were coming?"

"Over five hundred," Black said. "About a third

of those were planning on skiing in from the chateau. Otherwise, there wouldn't be enough parking."

"He's also got several luxury vans bringing up people."

"I know," Black said. "I considered posing as taxi drivers for the event, but I'm not sure I would've been able to stomach the drive back and forth all night. Plus, I'm sure we would've been more scrutinized at the gate."

"All I know is that if we go through all this trouble, Antoine better be here," she said. "I'm still not convinced Dr. Matthews has anything to do with this. As far as I can tell, he used the quest for the missing scientist as bait for Blunt."

"Don't worry. We'll figure out what's going on soon enough—as long as he doesn't kill us first."

The approaching vehicle slowed as Black stepped into the road and waved his hands in an effort to flag down the car. Smoke poured out from beneath the hood, drifting across both lanes of traffic. The car eased to a stop next to Black.

"What seems to be the problem?" a man asked in Italian. He was dressed in a tuxedo and was accompanied by a woman with a large sparkling diamond ring in the passenger side and a teenage girl in the back.

Bingo.

"Our car is broken down, and we're supposed to be catering at a party for the Duca's tonight," Black responded in Italian. "Would you mind giving us a lift? We can't miss work, especially a party for Mr. Duca."

The man glanced at the woman in the passenger seat, who nodded at him. "Okay, we'll take you in."

When they arrived at the gate, a guard asked to see their invitation. He examined it closely before handing it back. Then he inquired about their passengers.

"They are employees for the catering company," the man said.

The guard ordered Black and Shields to get out. After the car was waived through, the guard radioed to someone, requesting that they come help him at the entrance.

Shields nudged Black. "Let me take the lead on this one."

"It's all yours," he said as he stepped back.

"Sir, we're here with Bellisimo," she said in Italian, nodding in the direction of the catering company's van.

"I need to report this," he said. "No one enters this property without being cleared on our list. Your names weren't on it."

"That's because Mr. Duca requested extra workers at the last minute," she said. "I'm sure you'd hate to disappoint him."

"Hold on," he said. "Let me check." The guard stepped back and engaged someone on the same radio frequency in a conversation about how to handle the two Bellisimo employees.

Black eyed Shields closely and spoke in a hushed tone. "Are you sure this is going to work?"

"If it doesn't, I'll resort to tears," she whispered.

"I hope it doesn't come to that."

"Me, too," she said. "If you had any idea how much I hate having to conjure up tears."

As the man returned, he shook his head. "I'm sorry, but Luis, the catering director, is here on the premises and said he didn't know anything about a request for more workers at the last minute by Mr. Duca."

"This is outrageous," Black said as he started to walk around, flailing his arms and speaking in a loud voice. "We drove all the way up here, and then my car broke down, and now you're telling me there's no work? You tell Luis he needs to tell me to my face that I came all the way up here for no reason."

The man huffed and shook his head. Then Shields sprang into action, sobbing softly at first and then loudly.

"I need to pay rent, and if I don't work tonight, my daughter and I are going to be evicted from our apartment," she said.

The guard grinned wryly. "There are other ways

to make some quick money."

Black shoved the man. "Would you say that to Mr. Duca's daughter? Call Luis now."

The guard radioed for Luis to come outside. While they waited, the man watched both of them, checking for any illegal objects. Shields set off the alarm as it whooped in wild fashion.

He scowled and she lifted her pants leg, revealing her prosthetic.

"Sorry, ma'am," he said. "I didn't know."

She shrugged. "Happens all the time."

Moments later, a bald man wearing a furrowed brow twaddled toward the gate.

"What's this all about?" shouted Luis, as he wiped his hands on a towel. He was flanked by a pair of servers. "I don't have time for this. I don't know these people, and Mr. Duca never requested any more workers."

Upon reaching Black and Shields, Luis set his jaw and shook his head.

"I'm sorry, sir, but Georgio sent us," Black said, referencing Bellisimo's owner. "Here's the letter he handed us this morning."

Black handed the faked document over to Luis for inspection. Researching the best way to get onto Duca's estate in time for his daughter's grand party, Shields had managed to get a copy of the owner's signature on his letterhead through some publicly available documents. She forged the letter and used her hacking skills to re-route all his calls and texts to a burner phone.

After perusing the letter, he pulled out his cell. "Let me check with my boss."

Half a minute later, he returned with a shrug. "This is from my boss. I would know that signature anywhere."

"And?" the guard asked.

"And he's not responding," Luis said.

"What do you want to do?"

"Would you go against your boss's wishes?" Luis asked the guard.

He shook his head. "Absolutely not."

"Neither do I. I'll assign them to stay with me just to be sure. I know how careful you are with security."

The guard nodded and gestured for them to follow Luis. As Black and Shields fell in line behind Luis, he explained how the evening was supposed to go and what they would be doing. But Black was hardly listening. He was scanning the area for signs of Antoine.

After half an hour of chopping vegetables, Black excused himself to use the restroom. Night had fallen, and more guests had poured into Duca's mansion. They were still enjoying the hors d'oeuvres in anticipation of the evening's meal. As Black was walking around, he noticed Antoine at the back of the room.

When Black returned to the kitchen, he told Shields they needed to go.

She walked out onto the floor and over to Antoine. "Excuse me, sir, but Mr. Duca would like to speak with you in the back."

Antoine pointed at his chest and furrowed his brow. "Me?"

Shields nodded. "Right this way, please."

She led him down a long corridor before ushering him toward a hallway on the right. He glanced down it and then darted straight ahead.

Black, who'd been waiting in the shadows, let out a string of expletives and then raced after Antoine. The assassin was leaping over a balcony when Black exited the house. In an effort to keep eyes on the target, Black followed suit, jumping blindly over the edge and trusting that Antoine knew what he was doing.

Black sank into the fresh snow and could see Antoine a few meters ahead, slogging through the powder. Seconds later, Antoine picked up speed before he sprinted toward a nearby shed that was covered with skiing and snowboarding gear. Antoine secured some straps around his shoes and took off on a board.

As the ground hardened beneath Black's feet, he picked up steam and continued pursuit. By the time he reached the shed, Antoine already had a twenty-meter head start and was gaining more ground every second.

"Come on, Black," Shields said over their coms. "I'll meet you at the bottom." She raced toward the gate and disappeared into the night.

Black tightened the bindings and shoved off, zooming down the hill in search of Antoine. The path twisted around the mountain and reconnected with the nearby Celeste Ski Resort. Lighted paths made it easier to navigate, but Black struggled to locate Antoine. Moments later, Black heard some young people shouting and shaking their fists as a man in a dark jacket zoomed past them.

Gotcha!

Black zeroed in on Antoine, who started to wobble. While Black was certain Antoine had been on a snowboard before, he hadn't been on one in a while. Black found the fastest line behind Antoine and closed in on him. Antoine looked over his shoulder and made eye contact with Black. Instead of staying the course, Antoine dashed toward a clump of trees and disappeared. Seconds later, Black sped into the trees and was summarily knocked to the ground. He looked up to find Antoine towering overhead.

"What took you so long to find me?" he asked with a sly grin.

CHAPTER 9

**National Personnel Records Center
St. Louis, Missouri**

BLUNT STRODE INTO the front doors of the National Personnel Records Center, emptied his pockets, and placed everything in his hands on the x-ray machine's conveyor belt. The guard on duty nodded at Blunt's shoes. But instead of removing them, he held up his security badge. The guard shrugged.

"I don't care who you work for. Everybody has to take off their shoes to get past me," he said.

"That's not a wise idea," Blunt said. "Dr. Sholls can't even help me. You're going to regret this in about ten seconds."

The guard rolled his eyes as he pulled up on his holster, the leather creaking as he did.

"Don't say you weren't warned," Blunt said.

Blunt adhered to strict hygienic guidelines, even for his feet. But removing his shoes in public was a pet peeve. Modern technology had long since eliminated the need to take them off and have them x-rayed, but it was a practice still common at most airports.

He begrudgingly complied. The guard smirked as he watched Blunt.

When Blunt finished, he collected his visitor's pass and trudged down the hall. A few minutes later, he was speaking with one of the archivists in the special collections section, inquiring about where he might be able to find some war records from Vietnam. She helped Blunt find all the corresponding numbers to locate the files he was after. Once he turned in his request slip, he went to the cafeteria and bought a cup of coffee while he waited for the first set of returns.

"How are we looking?" Blunt asked in his coms after a half hour.

"So far, so good," answered Alex Duncan, another Firestorm handler. Alex primarily worked with agent Brady Hawk, but on occasion she helped Blunt with some of his side projects.

"Let me know when you think I should head back upstairs," he said.

"Any time now is great," she said. "I'm sending the schematics to your phone along with directions on how to reach the section with all the sealed files."

"I'm on my way," Blunt said as he lumbered

toward the elevators.

"You know, you've got to be about the most unassuming operative ever," Alex said.

"That's right. I'm just an old fart gathering some research."

"Okay, the archivists will be delivering all the requested documents in ten minutes. Once that happens, they'll gather all the new requests made in the last hour and go get those. I'll loop the security footage after the archivists leave, and you'll be on your own. Think you can handle that?"

"Of course," he said.

"The microdot tracker you placed on your request form enabled me to give you the exact location where all the sealed files are stored. You'll have to hustle. Do you have the card I gave you?"

"Retrieved it from my shoe in the restroom earlier this morning," Blunt said.

"Sounds like you're all set. Just wait for my signal."

Blunt ambled up to the desk and waited for the archivists to return with the boxes of information he'd requested. After five minutes, several workers paraded out push carts leaden with gray boxes containing records of military personnel for the various researchers. Blunt took his boxes and spread them out on a table. Ten minutes later, the archivists collected all the latest request slips and disappeared again.

"You're up," Alex said.

Blunt crept up to the door and waved his access card in front of the security pad. The lock clicked, and he tugged the door open. He walked down a long hallway before entering a vast room where files were arranged in an alpha-numeric system. Using the file Alex had sent, he meandered toward the back where a large enclosed room housed all the sealed files. He shook his head as he stared at the shelves packed with files.

The secrets contained in here.

"How am I doing, Alex?" Blunt asked.

He waited for her reply, but she didn't answer.

"Alex, do you copy?"

Still nothing.

Blunt cursed under his breath and looked at the numbers on the file from his phone. With the special system, he needed a few minutes to figure out how it worked. Once he did, he walked down the center aisle and located the file on the bottom of a shelf near the end of the row.

"Hello?" called a woman.

Blunt swallowed hard before whispering, "Alex, can you hear me?"

Nothing.

His palms started sweating as he heard echoing

footsteps marching toward him.

Come on, come on.

"Is anyone else in here?" the woman asked again.

Blunt shuffled against the end of the row in an effort to avoid detection in case the prying archivist made a horizontal sweep along the rows.

Then the noise stopped.

He exhaled slowly as the woman turned and headed back toward the door. Reverberating off the polished tile floor, the latch clicked open.

Blunt threw his head back in relief, resting it against the side of the shelves. She was gone.

Or was she?

He strained to hear more faint footfalls, wondering if they belonged to someone else outside the room or if the woman was moving more stealthily.

Blunt didn't want to find out, though he was certain that he couldn't stay hidden in the sealed files room much longer.

"Stop playing around, Chris," the woman said. "I know you're back here."

She edged closer.

Blunt's heart pounded.

CHAPTER 10

Merano, Italy

BLACK WINCED AND GRABBED his chest while lying on his back in the snow. The ice around him quickly chilled his body, while the blow he suffered left him in throbbing pain. Instead of celebrating Antoine's capture, Black had become a prisoner, staring up at the barrel of Antoine's pistol.

"Now I can send your boss the message I've been dying to give him," Antoine said.

"I can assure you that he isn't interested in talking with you," Black said as he grimaced while easing to his feet.

"Is that what he said?" Antoine asked.

"My boss is a man of few words," Black said.

"Just like I thought," Antoine said with a laugh. "What a coward. However, since you're so good at understanding what people are saying without actually saying it, I don't think you fully understand the kind of thing I want to communicate."

Black shrugged. "How difficult can it be? You want to kill me."

Antoine wagged his finger. "No, I want to sit down and talk with him. I need some answers."

"What kind of answers? You want to know why Blunt chose another operative over you?"

"I know why. I just want to hear him say it for myself. And then kill him. Now that I've captured one of his precious top assets, perhaps he'll be interested in listening."

Their conversation was interrupted when shouts and screams came from the distance. Antoine cursed as he turned to survey the scene.

"Trouble?" Black asked.

"For you and me both," Antoine said as he eyed his captive carefully. "Those are Duca's men out there, and if they catch us, they'll kill us both."

"I'm not so sure about that."

"This is one theory you don't want to try and disprove."

Black smirked. "So what do you want to do? Stay here and freeze to death? I'm not sure that's a good option for you either."

"Just keep your mouth shut," Antoine said, keeping his weapon trained on Black. "You are the one who created this mess by making such a scene at

Bella's party. And Mr. Duca isn't the kind of man to allow such interruptions to go unpunished."

They both sat quietly for the next half-hour until the men moved on to search higher up the mountain. Satisfied that it was safe to venture back onto the slopes again, Antoine explained how they would get to safety.

"There's a service trail we can get to easily from here," he said.

"And then what?" Black asked. "Are we going to walk back to Merano?"

"We'll walk down to the parking lot and borrow a car. When we get to the valley, we'll give your boss a call."

"This isn't going to end well for you," Black said.

"Says the man who's only a heartbeat away from his last breath. If I were you, I would take this moment to reflect on your good fortune and be thankful that you're still alive."

"Point the way," Black said.

Black and Antoine snowboarded to the service trail and then tossed their gear in the woods. As they trudged through the snow in silence, a voice pierced the air, causing both men to freeze.

"Drop the weapon," a woman said.

Black recognized Shields right away. He turned around and watched Antoine kneel and place his weapon on top of the snow.

"That's right," Shields said. "Now, hands in the air. You're coming with us."

"Not if I start shouting for help," Antoine said. "Duca's men will be crawling all over this place in a matter of seconds."

She shook her head. "Now why would you suggest doing a thing like that? I don't think Duca is your friend right now. Otherwise, you wouldn't have been hiding out for the last half-hour waiting for them to leave the area."

Antoine cursed as he followed Shields's commands. The trio continued on along the trail until they neared the parking lot. Black scanned the area and signaled that it was clear.

"Black, have I told you how much I hate the cold?" Shields asked. "This is insane. My leg is frozen now."

"Don't you mean legs?" Antoine asked with a furrowed brow.

She looked at Black. "Can I, just this once?"

"Just this once?" Black said with a stiff laugh followed by a shrug. "Why not?"

She didn't hesitate, spinning around and smashing the side of Antoine's head with her prosthetic and knocking him out.

"Yeah," she said with a chuckle. "Why not?"

Black heaved Antoine into the back of their car. "Now, it's time to get some answers."

CHAPTER 11

St. Louis, Missouri

BLUNT BRACED FOR his confrontation with the archivist. The last thing he wanted to do was hurt the woman, but he needed to see what was inside those files and who was using their office to protect themselves from high crimes. And he doubted she would just let him take a peek and forget that he was ever here. Blunt's palms beaded with sweat as the clicking of her heels sped up as she hustled down the row.

"Chris, I mean it," the woman said. "This isn't funny."

She was so close that Blunt could smell her flowery perfume. He kept his back to the shelf and edged slightly away from the end.

"Chris, I'm gonna—"

She stopped as a fire alarm blared in the room and warned all the archivists to exit immediately.

"This is a fire drill," said a woman's voice over the facility's intercom system. "All employees and guests please leave the premises immediately and report to the courtyard."

Blunt closed his eyes and steadied his breathing. He recognized the voice over the intercom as Alex's. If the scenario had been different, he would've smiled. But he scowled, his expression grave. Blunt was still in danger of getting caught as long as the archivist remained in the room.

The woman growled in frustration and hustled toward the entrance of the sealed records room.

"Chris, I'm waiting for you," she said.

Blunt didn't hear any more sounds for a few seconds before she spoke again.

"You're gonna pay for this," she said and exited the room, the door latching shut behind her.

Blunt exhaled and slumped against the end of the shelf.

Alex!

He waited a few seconds before carefully opening the folder. Without much time before everyone would return to the building, Blunt didn't even read the documents. Instead, he quickly flipped through the pages, stopping briefly to take a picture of each one. There were more than three dozen pages, all of which he was able to capture. He returned the papers into the file and re-sealed it.

Scrambling to his feet, Blunt hustled toward the exit. He kept his head down as he noticed all of the archivists had exited the floor. When he reached the security checkpoint, one worker remained, scanning all of the items going in and out the room.

"Sir, do you hear that fire alarm going off?" the guard asked.

Blunt nodded.

"You need to hustle more quickly next time. If that was a real fire, your life would be in danger."

"Sorry, I heard it was a drill—and I was in the can," Blunt said. "When nature calls…"

The guard rolled his eyes and waived Blunt through the turnstile. Once he reached the courtyard, all of the researchers were mingling with the archivists, all complaining about having to stand outside in the cold without having time to retrieve their jackets from the locker rooms.

Blunt didn't stop, maintaining his steady stride toward the parking lot. He had just cleared the plaza where everyone had congregated when someone called after him.

"Where are you going, sir?" asked a woman.

Blunt turned to see the archivist who'd helped him with his first pull of the morning.

"Oh, I think I've got everything I needed."

She smiled. "Oh, okay. You need to check your cart back in if you're finished."

"Would you be a dear and do it for me?" Blunt asked as he glanced at his watch. "I've got a pressing appointment, and I have no idea how much longer it'll take before we're allowed back inside."

"I'm sure I can handle that for you. Have a nice day, and thanks for visiting."

Blunt nodded and resumed his march toward his car.

"Nice work, sir," Alex said over the coms.

Blunt looked over his shoulder to make sure no one could hear him.

"What on earth happened?" he asked in a hushed tone.

"I don't know. The coms went dead for a while. I'm guessing that maybe you were in a section of the building where we couldn't get reception."

"I was starting to panic."

"That's understandable. I probably would be too if I was in that same situation, but I was monitoring you the whole time."

"Quick thinking about the fire alarms," Blunt said. "I swear that archivist was about six feet away from me."

"I'd guess maybe three feet," Alex said. "She was just around the corner from you when she spun and headed toward the door. We were very fortunate. Sorry to scare you like that, sir. It's not easy to hack into some of these government facilities, even when you know what you're doing."

"I'm just glad nobody saw me."

"Roger that," she said. "Did you get what you were looking for?"

"I'll know in a minute once I look through them," Blunt said. "I didn't have a chance to read anything as I was just taking pictures as fast as I could."

"Okay. Well, safe travels back to Washington."

"Thanks, Alex."

Blunt hung up and walked toward his car. Once he reached it, he climbed inside and immediately opened the sealed file of Capt. Black.

Blunt found the incident in question and started carefully reading the report. He found the man who gave the order for Capt. Black's mission and directed the record to be sealed.

Blunt's mouth fell agape as he stared at the page.

CHAPTER 12

Somewhere over the Atlantic Ocean

THE KC-130 SHIMMIED as the plane withstood a long stretch of turbulence. Black looked at Shields in the bench seat next to him, her knuckles turning white as she tightened her grip on the edge of her seat. With eyes glazed over and focused on the floor, she appeared pale and on the verge of throwing up.

"I thought you liked flying," Black said, his voice vibrating as the plane shook.

"Not like this," she said, her gaze unbroken.

Black tried to suppress a smile forming across his lips. "So, you only enjoy traveling in one of Blunt's luxury jets?"

"Considering that my teeth are rattling out of my mouth and we're babysitting this lunatic, I don't think it should come as a surprise that I'd rather fly any other way but by strapping myself into a KC-130 to get across the Atlantic."

Black shrugged. "I tried to convince Blunt otherwise, but he said that because we were transporting a prisoner for the CIA, we had to use military transportation."

Shields grunted and closed her eyes. "This is why I could never be a soldier. There's just no reason anyone ever needs to be subjected to something like this."

"Would you like for me to get you a paper sack for your nausea?" he asked.

"I will stomp on your foot. And let me assure you that carbon fiber and titanium don't feel all that great when smashed on your toes."

Black withdrew. "How about I just take your word for it?"

She cast a sideways glance at him before peeking at Antoine, who was chained to his seat across from them.

"What did Blunt tell you about me?" Antoine asked. "I know you had to speak with him."

Black cocked his head to one side and scowled. "Are you really that concerned about what people think about you? That's generally not a trait I've seen associated with most assassins I've come across."

"I couldn't care less what people think about me," Antoine said with a snarl. "But I don't like being vilified and framed."

"Your own government did that to you, according to Blunt," Shields said.

"What else did he tell you? That I kill for sport?"

"Something like that," Black said.

"Well, ask Blunt what other kind of things he asked me to do," Antoine said. "The truth is he tried to get me to clean up one of his messes. He used me and then to keep my mouth shut put me on every watch list on the planet."

"Is that why you have to resort to relying on the mafia to keep you hidden?" Shields asked.

Antoine shook his head. "My relationship with Mr. Duca goes back a long time."

"But he was still going to kill you?" she asked.

"You don't understand, though I'm not sure I can expect you to if you've never had any dealings with Duca. There are certain areas you don't mess with—and one of those is his daughter. If he would've caught me, he would've held me responsible for leading you to his estate and ultimately ruining his daughter's party."

"Sounds like a great family guy," Black said.

"I know you're joking, but he puts his family above his own mafia family," Antoine said. "I once saw him stab his top lieutenant in the neck after he criticized Duca's son for his performance in a soccer match. Everyone watched the guy bleed out on the floor. Then Duca turned to all the people in the room and warned them that this is what happens to anyone who speaks ill of his children."

"You're saying that with a hint of admiration in your voice," Shields said.

"I admire a man who operates out of conviction."

Black chuckled. "No wonder it's come to this for you. You're a soul without a compass."

"Don't act like you're morally superior," Antoine said. "I've heard about some of the things you've done."

"The justice I exact for my country is deserved," Black said.

"Is it really?" Antoine asked as he laughed softly. "That's exactly what I would expect someone like you to say. You ride around on your high horse as if the rest of the world is morally bankrupt, all the while ignoring every—"

Antoine stopped talking, and his stare went blank he swayed back and forth. After a moment, he went limp and fell to his left. His head came to rest on the seat two spots away. A beeping noise went off, alerting them that something was wrong.

"What is that?" Shields asked.

"An alarm of some sort," Black said.

"I know that," she said, throwing her hands in

the air. "I want to know where it's coming from."

Shields turned her head so it was facing the front of the plane and leaned toward Antoine's position.

"What do you hear?" Black asked.

"It sounds like it's coming from Antoine."

They both unbuckled and rushed over to him. Black knelt next to their captive and checked his pulse, while Shields checked his pants.

"What are you looking for?" Black asked.

"His blood sugar monitor," Shields said. "He told us that he was a diabetic when we were searching him earlier."

"I can't believe I forgot."

"That's why we're a team," she said. "Now go get him some water, and see if you can find something for him to eat over there."

Black went over to Shields's pack, found a water bottle and a granola bar, and then hustled back to her.

"This ought to do the trick," she said as she snatched the snack from him and peeled it open.

Black splashed some water in Antoine's face. "Are you all right?"

Antoine slowly rose. "I'd be a lot better off if I wasn't chained to a chair in a U.S. military transport plane."

"The alarm on your monitor went off," Shields said. "Drink some of this water and eat this."

Antoine sat up groggily and followed her instructions, shoveling the food into his mouth.

"All better?" she asked.

"I'm getting there," he said between mouthfuls. "I'm just glad I was with you two when this happened. Blunt would've let me die."

"Enough with the commentary," Black said.

"Did you look up Blue Moon Rising Enterprises like I told you to?"

Black shook his head. "I'm not interested in getting into this kind of game with you."

Antoine shook his head. "All I'm saying is that you should know what kind of man you're working for, that's all."

Black and Shields returned to their seats and rode along in silence. But the thoughts in Black's head were deafening. He wanted to think he could trust Blunt fully, but Black started to wonder.

And he wasn't going to rest easy until he found the truth.

"I need to make a call," Black said.

"Who?"

"An old friend who might be able to help me get to the bottom of this thing."

CHAPTER 13

Washington, D.C.

BLUNT AWOKE TO LOUD rapping on his door just after 6:30 a.m. He stumbled out of bed and threw on a housecoat before lumbering downstairs. Muttering a few choice words, he shuffled down the hallway and checked his security monitor before answering.

"Don't you think it's a little early to be making house calls?" Blunt said after opening the door.

Robert Besserman, dressed in a dark suit, held out a cup of coffee. "A peace offering?"

"Get inside," Blunt said, waving Besserman into the house and then taking the drink.

Besserman followed Blunt into the kitchen where the two men sat at the bar.

"What's this all about?" Blunt said. "I can't imagine it's good news."

Besserman sighed and shook his head. "This

couldn't wait."

"You're starting to worry me, Bobby. Just spit it out."

"Elliott is about to go public with the hearing," Besserman said. "According to one of my sources at the capitol building, he's gathering sworn affidavits and is putting you at the center of his crosshairs. He's planning on springing a few surprise questions when you take the stand."

Blunt took a long sip of his coffee. "There's no way I'm taking the stand. That'd be lunacy."

"I know that's not ideal, but if you don't, it's only going to make you look guilty of the exact thing Elliott claims is going on."

"Wilson Wellington," Blunt muttered. "That guy has a closet full of skeletons."

"More like a garage full. But he's been airing his dirty laundry for a while now and is on some crusade to expose his past deeds to show how he's reformed."

"He's just trying to keep his seat. That guy is more slippery than a pocket full of pudding."

"Apparently, there are people who are buying it, mainly the voters in his district. You'll have to dig deep to unearth something he hasn't been honest about. Most of what he's revealed about his past is just low-level corruption that almost every member of congress is guilty of at some point."

Blunt huffed a laugh through his nose. "That shouldn't be too hard to do."

"Well, if you're going to leverage that into stopping the hearing, you better do it quick before these details about what Elliott plans to do are leaked to the media. From what I understand, he also has a surprise witness that's going to bring down everything."

"A surprise witness?" Blunt asked as he narrowed his eyes. "That's not how hearings are supposed to work."

"Of course not, but when Wilson Wellington is orchestrating things behind the scenes, all bets are off."

"Who could he possibly trot out there? A disgruntled operative? I've ticked some people off in my day, but not by doing anything nefarious. They'd be opening up a can of worms if they want to put the intelligence community on trial."

"Which is why everyone has been working tirelessly to put an end to this charade," Besserman said. "But all that pressure has made Elliott dig his heels in deeper. And now we're at a point where some operations are going to be very disrupted, if not exposed, if we don't figure out a way to end this. Unfortunately, you're at ground zero on all of this."

"So, you're telling me I need to stop this?"

Besserman nodded. "We've done just about all we can do, applying as much pressure as possible to Elliott."

"Maybe that's your problem," Blunt said. "You're going after the wrong guy. Wellington is the one who can end it."

"We've tried, but he seems impervious at the moment to any accusations levied against him."

"Don't worry," Blunt said. "I've got something that will make him stop in his tracks."

"And if he doesn't?"

"Then we're all screwed."

CHAPTER 14

**Undisclosed location
outside Washington, D.C.**

BLUNT WASN'T A STRANGER to CIA black sites, but this was one he'd never been to before—or at least if he had, he didn't remember it. He sat in the far back seat of the black SUV and spoke in hushed tones with his escort, Robert Besserman.

"Are you sure you want to see Antoine?" Besserman asked.

"I don't think I'd spit on him if he was on fire after the kind of trouble he's caused me," Blunt said. "But we were tasked with finding Dr. Matthews, and I need to know if that was some ruse or if he's still alive. I owe it to his daughter to find out since every other organization has abandoned the search for him."

"And if Antoine was just playing you, then what?"

"I don't know. Put him in a dark hole in the ground or turn him over to Interpol? Makes no difference to me. He's been a problem for numerous intelligence agencies around the world, so I'm sure any one of them would relish the opportunity to extract a pound of flesh from him."

Their vehicle ground to a halt just outside the gate. The guard inspected their documents before waving the pair inside.

"Just don't make it personal," Besserman said. "I've heard Antoine has quite a way of manipulating people."

"Don't worry," Blunt said. "I know all his mind games. After all, I was the one who taught them to him."

Blunt entered the interrogation room where Antoine sat with his hands chained to the desk in front of him. He didn't even glance at Blunt as he entered the room, instead staring at the two-way mirror.

"If you wanted to talk, you could've just called," Blunt said as he settled into the chair across from Antoine.

Antoine narrowed his eyes as he turned his gaze toward Blunt. "Do you think this is some kind of joke? Because I can assure you that it isn't."

"I know you tried to kill one of my agents."

Antoine looked down at his hand and shook his head. "I'm exactly where I want to be."

"Then perhaps you should reassess your life goals."

"Do you think I'm going to let you get away with what you did?" Antoine asked as he glared at Blunt.

"I didn't do anything," Blunt said. "You were the one who decided to take justice into your own hands."

"That problem needed to be dealt with—those were your words, not mine."

"I never gave you an order. I was simply venting frustration."

"To an operative vying for a job with your agency, that sounded like a directive."

Blunt sighed. "I'm sorry you interpreted things that way. This organization wasn't designed to pick off political enemies for me or anyone else. It was created to protect the country's interests."

"And you're the one who gets to determine that without anyone watching over your shoulder? What a farce."

"I've never operated within a vacuum. The fact that you think so shows just how little you know about me. You were a great agent, but you have let the freedom you were given go to your head. And now, you're done."

"That's what you—"

Antoine failed to finish his sentence, instead doubling over in pain. He slumped to the floor, his hands still tethered to the table.

"Guard!" Blunt said. "Get in here quick. This man needs some medical attention."

A pair of guards rushed into the room and began

inspecting Antoine. Blunt stepped back and took in the scene. The device attached to Antoine's belt started beeping.

"He's diabetic," Blunt said, remembering that fact about the aspiring Firestorm operative. "Check his blood sugar levels."

One of the men inspected the readout on Antoine's belt and then rushed out of the room. Moments later, the guard returned with a candy bar, a piece already halfway unwrapped.

"Here," he said, handing the snack to Antoine. "Eat this."

Antoine gobbled it up and remained on the floor for a couple minutes, holding his head in his hands. After he looked up, he checked his device again.

"All better," he said as he eased back into his seat.

The guards nodded and then exited the room, leaving Blunt alone with Antoine again.

"Before you pass out on me again, I need some answers," Blunt said.

"How about no," Antoine said.

"Cute," Blunt said. "Now, where's Dr. Matthews?"

"You think I'm just going to give out that information without some sort of quid pro quo?"

"If you're not willing to work with me, I can't help you."

"You are going to help me?"

"Maybe," Blunt said. "As it stands right now, information about Dr. Matthews's whereabouts is your only bargaining chip. Use it wisely or you may get stuck in here."

"If you think that's my only leverage, you're sorely mistaken," Antoine said. "I know all about Blue Moon Rising. It's going to be the end of you."

Blunt shook his head. "I don't care what you think you know about that, it's wrong. And if you believe that's going to help you get out of this predicament, you're gambling with your life."

Antoine shrugged. "Maybe I'll just let the public decide."

"Good luck with that," Blunt said as he stood. He ambled over to the door, knocked on it, calling for the guards. "Whenever you're ready to talk about Dr. Matthews's location, I'll be ready to listen."

"Maybe we'll do it in person since I'll be out of here before you know it," Antoine said.

Blunt chuckled. "You truly are delusional, Antoine. Have a nice life."

"You're going to pay for everything you've done by the time I'm finished," Antoine said, calling after Blunt.

"Goodbye, Antoine," Blunt said just before the door slammed shut behind him.

Besserman was waiting in the corridor outside the interrogation room. "How'd it go?"

"I'm not sure he knows anything about Dr. Matthews," Blunt said. "If he does, he isn't saying. That's going to cost him dearly if I learn otherwise."

Besserman nodded. "We'll try some other methods to get that intel out of him, but I'm not making any promises."

"I understand. Just do the best you can."

Blunt ambled back to the car. He had work to do, especially regarding Blue Moon Rising.

How did Antoine even know about that?

CHAPTER 15

Washington, D.C.

BLUNT YANKED OPEN THE DOOR to the restaurant 1789 and strode up to the host stand. He didn't have a reservation nor did he want one. While Blunt was hungry, he wasn't here to eat. One of Senator Wilson Wellington's new assistants had been far more forthcoming with her boss's schedule than she should've been when Blunt inquired.

Wellington is going to hate this.

The thought made Blunt smile as he asked about Wellington's whereabouts from the young man at the lectern doling out seating assignments for each dining party.

"The senator and his guest are in the corner," the man said, nodding toward the back. "But he didn't say anything about anyone else joining them."

Blunt shrugged and patted the host on the shoulder. "Maybe it slipped his mind."

Wellington was seated in a booth with a shapely blonde woman some thirty years his junior. He swilled his wine, smelled it, and then crinkled up his nose before handing the glass back to the waiter.

"It's chilled too much for my liking," Wellington said. "Take it back. Bring me back one of your French merlots not a degree cooler than sixty-three. Is that understood?"

"Yes, sir," the waiter said before hustling away with the bottle.

Blunt marched up to the table, wearing a faint smile. While he wanted to punch Wellington in the face, Blunt hadn't become successful in Washington without learning to be diplomatic.

"Well, if it isn't my favorite cowboy," Wellington said, offering his hand to Blunt.

Blunt took the senator's hand and nodded politely at Katrina Rutherford, the socialite who was at the center of Wellington's marital scandal several years earlier and was dubbed the "marriage wrecker" by New York tabloids. Including Wellington, she had broken up four D.C. power couples and was unapologetic about it. However, Wellington was the first one she'd decided to settle down with. She tilted her head to one side and mirrored his gesture. And Wellington, ever the spin doctor, had turned his marriage to the beauty into a positive moment in his political career, deploying her to reach out to younger disenfranchised voters. The move had helped him solidify the grip he had on his seat.

"I don't know how many times I've told you, Wilson, but being from Texas doesn't make you a cowboy," Blunt said.

Wellington withdrew. "You say that as if you act like I made a disparaging comment. You know I love those Texas ranchers. In fact, I'm about to enjoy the fruits of their labor with a nice filet mignon served with my wine."

"They do raise the best cattle there," Blunt said. "But I didn't come here to talk with you about choice cuts."

"Then, please, tell me why you're here, because my lovely bride and I have a lot to catch up on after her recent trip to Naples," Wellington said.

"Are you sure you want her to stick around for this?"

"Of course," Wellington said. "Anything you have to say to me, you can say in front of her."

Blunt shifted his weight from one foot to the other, tapping the file folder in his hands against his leg. "I just wanted to ask you to rein in Allan Elliott and have him stop this ridiculous hearing."

Wellington cautiously eyed Blunt and waited a moment before responding. "Do you have something to hide, J.D.?"

"I haven't done anything I'm ashamed of, if that's what you mean," Blunt said. "I've only done what my country has asked me to do."

"Then why are you so worried?"

"Some valuable assets will have their covers blown if this circus is allowed to take place. And you have the power to shut down Elliott's witch hunt before it gets started."

The waiter returned to the table, pushing a cart with a wine bottle nestled in an iced pitcher. "I'm sorry. Am I interrupting anything?"

"Nah," Wellington said as he scribbled something on a napkin and handed it to Blunt. "Just signing an autograph for a big fan."

Blunt stepped back to allow the waiter access to the table. He poured a glass of merlot for Wellington, who immediately screwed up his face and puckered his lips after tasting the drink. He placed the wine stem on the table and dismissed the glass with a wave of the back of his hand.

"I thought I said sixty-three degrees," Wellington said. "That was at least fifty degrees. Far too cold for any proper wine serving."

The waiter maintained a straight face before rolling away the cart.

"Would you drink wine that was fifty degrees?" Wellington asked Blunt.

"I wouldn't drink it at any temperature."

Wellington pointed at Blunt. "You see, this is why we don't get along. You don't even drink wine. That's just preposterous."

Blunt flung down the folder on the table. "Not nearly as preposterous as this."

"What's that?" Wellington asked, nodding at the documents.

"It's for your reading pleasure, the kind of thing that will end up ruining your political aspirations, no matter how you try to spin it," Blunt said. "Maybe you and Katrina can read it together."

Wellington huffed and shook his head. "Tell me what I'm looking at."

"Documents that every news media outlet will have if you don't stop Elliott's hearing tomorrow."

"There isn't anything in there that's even worth looking at since I don't have any skeletons in my closet," Wellington said before leaning back in his seat and interlocking his fingers behind his head.

"Perhaps I should read something from this quote about you, Colonel Wellington," Blunt said. He picked up the documents and turned to a page near the back.

"Is this really necessary?" Wellington asked.

Blunt ignored him before reading a passage aloud. "Col. Wellington ordered Capt. Black to fly over the area that was designated as a no-fly zone, according to Capt. Miller and Capt. Braxton. The two pilots pleaded with Col. Wellington to rescind his order, but he refused."

"And the investigation into the matter found no wrong doing on my part," Wellington said.

Blunt shrugged. "Is that going to matter when the media gets a hold of this? They're going to cast you as the one who pulled the trigger on a decorated war hero."

"There's a perfectly rational explanation for all of this, one that I would think someone from the intelligence community could appreciate," Wellington said. "But apparently you're not as concerned with keeping secrets as you claim to be."

"Put an end to Elliott's hearing, or we'll let the public decide about your actions."

"You think Elliott's my puppet?"

"He'll listen to you," Blunt said, "especially since you were the one who put him up to this."

"This is getting more outlandish by the minute."

"Is it? Or do you find that the truth stings?"

Wellington shook his index finger at Blunt. "First of all, I never put Elliott up to anything. And secondly, these files you dug up on me don't amount to much dirt, at least the kind that puts politicians on the defensive. It's easy to explain why I did what I did, especially in the heat of war."

"Then why were these records sealed?"

Wellington set his jaw but didn't answer.

"Exactly," Blunt said. "You don't have an answer for that, at least one that anybody is going to believe."

After a few moments of silence, Wellington spoke. "I'll consider your request."

"Thank you," Blunt said. He pointed at the folder on the table. "You can have that. I have plenty of copies, all ready to go out in the mail first thing in the morning. You have until 10:00 p.m. tonight to decide what you want to do."

Blunt spun and walked toward the door, confident Wellington would acquiesce to the demands.

But if he didn't?

Blunt wasn't sure he had any other options—and that idea scared the hell out of him.

CHAPTER 16

TITUS BLACK ADJUSTED his wig and then fixed his fake mustache. While looking like Thomas Magnum wasn't all bad, Black hated how the appliqué made his upper lip itch. He checked himself once more in the mirror before climbing out of his car and heading inside Off the Record, his favorite bar to eavesdrop for Washington gossip before he supposedly died. He usually went in disguise, but walking in without one would make people think they'd seen a ghost, not to mention igniting rumors that he was still alive.

As a favorite hangout spot for prominent lawmakers and media members, Off the Record was tucked beneath the Hay-Adams hotel just a half-block from the White House. Black descended the steps and scanned the room. It didn't take him long to find Melissa Nash, a family friend who'd ascended the ranks at the CIA to become one of the agency's top analysts. She tucked her straight, brown hair behind her ears and looked up. Her eyes lit up when she saw Black.

"Mr. Jackson," she said, standing up and offering her hand.

"Please, just call me Luke," Black said with a subtle wink. "Can I buy you another drink?"

"Of course," she said. "I'm drinking a gin and tonic."

Black signaled for the waitress, who came over and took his drink orders before scurrying off to the bar.

"It's so good to see you," she said. "I didn't think I'd ever see you again."

"Well, don't believe everything you read. We'll have to catch up at a different time, maybe in a more secure location. But this couldn't wait."

"I understand," she said, sliding her hand across the table and touching his. He also felt the small device she jammed under his fingertips. "Just being cautious."

"Of course," Black said. "Anything else I should know about the information contained on here?"

She shook her head. "I don't make judgments. That's your job. I just find what I find and let you put the pieces together. That's what you're best at. But everything should be in there for you to figure out what's what."

Black nodded and eased the flash drive into his pocket. "For what it's worth, Melissa, I'm sorry I couldn't tell you the truth about what happened. I know that—"

She held up her hand. "No need to apologize. We're in the same line of work. And I think it's safe to say that we understand both the risks involved as well as the limitations on what can be said. It's why we could never be together."

"I do wish things could've been different."

She shrugged. "We both chose this life. And we knew the sacrifice that went along with it. No need to pine over the past."

Black nodded. "Thanks for this. I have to get going."

He threw a fifty dollar bill on the table and stood.

"Be careful," she said. "What I found, there are some powerful people connected to that group. If you start poking around—"

Her words trailed off, her insinuation clear.

"I'll watch my back," he said. "And thanks for the heads up."

Black spun toward the door and sauntered off. He drove straight to Shields's apartment, accessing her place through a private elevator on the lower deck of the parking garage. She was sipping a cup of tea while leaning against her kitchen counter when he walked in.

"What'd she give you?" she asked.

"This flash drive," he said, holding up the device. "She said all the information on here should help us make a decision about what to do."

"And she didn't tell you anything one way or the other?"

Black shook his head. "Melissa's an analyst. She looks at the data. According to her, that's all she does."

"I know that's a lie," Shields said.

"Well, that's what she said. But she also issued a warning that the people connected with Blue Moon Rising were powerful people and to be careful."

Shields held her hand out. "Enough talk. Let's see what's on there."

Black placed the flash drive in her hand, and then she jammed the device into the side port on her laptop. Then she clicked on a folder and scanned a list of files. One by one, Shields clicked on them. After perusing the data on the first few spreadsheets, she whistled.

"Look at this," she said, pointing at the screen. "There's a lot of money running through this company."

"No kidding," Black said. "So, where's it going?"

"Private bank accounts in the Cayman Islands, according to this corresponding file," she said.

"That doesn't exactly tell us anything," he said.

"Blue Moon is giving money to people who don't want anyone to know they're getting money. Certainly not a novel idea, nor is it criminal."

Shields gasped. "Wait a minute. Look at this name."

Black squinted at the small font on the screen, peering closer to it. He furrowed his brow. "I don't recognize that one."

"You don't?" Shields asked, her fingers flying furiously on the keyboard. "Check this out." She hit the return key and tilted the screen toward Black.

Black's eyes widened. "Oh, now that is a name I'm familiar with—Andrei Orlovsky."

"Yep, Andrew Olson is the alias he uses during his transactions with the West."

Black shook his head. "What on Earth would Blunt be funneling money to Orlovsky for?"

"It's not just Blunt," she said. "He's not the only one whose name is listed on the articles of incorporation."

Black scanned the list. "What are we getting ourselves into here?"

"I don't know," Shields said, "but I'm not sure this helps us get to the bottom of anything."

Black sighed. "Maybe the bottom of some muddied waters. I've got an uneasy feeling about this."

"That makes two of us," Shields said.

CHAPTER 17

BLUNT PACED AROUND his library, gnawing on a cigar. He checked his watch, and it was two minutes before the deadline he'd given Sen. Wellington. As someone with aspirations of ascending to the highest office in the land, Wellington would struggle to weather a political storm that cast him as a nefarious military commander. The public sentiment toward the military was a mixed bag. The overwhelming majority of the American people were proud of their soldiers, but there was a vocal minority who felt the military was full of corrupt leaders after a rash of scandals. And the loudest of those people all seemed to occupy seats behind news desks on just about every cable television network. Risking such a story breaking as Capitol Hill swirled with rumors that Wellington had formed an exploratory committee regarding the upcoming election could torpedo his run before it ever got off the ground.

Blunt received a text from Besserman asking if there was any news to report.

"None yet," Blunt wrote back.

He resumed strolling around his office, checking his phone every few seconds. It was set to vibrate but he couldn't help himself. Blunt's next move wasn't certain. He couldn't afford to put the intelligence community under such an intense microscope, but that seemed like a foregone conclusion if Wellington didn't acquiesce to Blunt's threat. Elliott's hearing was scheduled to start in less than thirty-six hours with no procedural way to shut it down. And if Blunt opted to move forward and expose Wellington, the fallout could be twice as bad. However, Blunt clung to the hope that the media and the public outcry over Wellington's abhorrent actions while serving in the military would attract the most headlines.

A quarter of an hour went by before Blunt's phone finally rang. The caller ID showed up as unknown.

This had better be Wellington.

"The deadline was fifteen minutes ago," Blunt said as he answered the phone.

"I had to do my due diligence," Wellington said. "But based on my conclusion, I wasn't too worried about missing the deadline."

"I thought you wanted to be President."

"I still will be—and I'll make my first campaign promise right now: I promise to make your life a living hell."

Blunt grunted and then huffed a laugh through his nose. "That'll look great on t-shirts and bumper stickers. Funny thing is, it's probably the truth—not just for me but for all Americans."

"You'll be in prison long before that," Wellington said.

"There are a couple of problems with that claim, starting with the fact that I haven't done anything wrong. You're also forgetting that I know some pretty powerful people who have the ability to squash any trumped-up accusations you try to throw at me."

"You should know by now that not everything has to be true to inflict the necessary damage."

Blunt examined his cigar before setting it down on the edge of his desk. "I shouldn't have to remind you that I know how the game is played. I did it for quite a while on Capitol Hill. So, if you want to come after me, I suggest you come with more than just empty threats."

"J.D., I wasn't born yesterday. I know how you got those personnel records."

"Oh really?"

"All I had to do was put two and two together," Wellington said. "An unexpected fire drill at the

Military Personnel Records Center just days before you waved those documents in my face. That was kind of sloppy work, though that's what happens when guilty people start to get anxious about a reckoning. And that's what Elliott is bringing, isn't it? And it's long overdue for an intelligence community that is operating unchecked and out of control."

"You have a fanciful imagination, not to mention a gross misperception about how the intelligence community operates, which is kind of surprising coming from you since you've been in Washington long enough and served in the military. You should know that what we do is always in the best interest of our country."

Wellington chuckled. "Sometimes. There are other occasions where you're engaging in a pet project for one of our own power-hungry leaders. And it's all recognized as legal. That's something I intend to change."

"The irony of that statement isn't lost on me."

"I don't care what you think about it," Wellington said. "It's the truth. And I'm going to make sure everybody knows about what you and your ilk does."

"And what exactly am I doing?" Blunt asked. He needed to make sure that word hadn't leaked about his involvement with Firestorm.

"You're thriving in the shadows—and I'm going

to drag you into the light."

He doesn't know a thing.

Blunt picked up his cigar and popped it back into his mouth. "It's your career, Senator. Hope you've enjoyed it while it lasted."

Blunt hung up the phone and scrolled through his contacts. He needed to make a call. Wellington had left no other options.

CHAPTER 18

ALLISON CARTER'S NIGHTLY TV SHOW ranked among the highest rated in the cable news network world. On The Carter Connection, she interviewed policy makers, movers, and shakers according to the tagline used to promote her program. The former New York beauty queen didn't mind mixing it up with Washington's elite on air, using her platform to challenge lawmakers to bring about reform in areas seemingly ignored by Congress.

She had just finished wrapping up her program for the evening and was removing her jewelry when her cell phone vibrated across the dressing room counter. The number wasn't one she recognized, which was the norm. Tired and ready to go home, she almost sent the call straight to voicemail but decided against it and answered.

"How are you, Allison? This is J.D. Blunt," said the caller.

"Senator Blunt—"

"Former senator now," he corrected.

"Well, you'll always be my favorite Texas senator. Now, what can I do for you?"

"I need your help."

"My help?" she asked. "Weren't you recently tabbed by Washington Whispers as the most powerful man behind the scenes in the city?"

"That was five years ago—and I'm hardly behind the scenes."

"If you're doing anything, I sure haven't heard about it," she said as she stood and then exited the room.

"I'm certainly not an invalid, but I don't have quite the sway I used to have."

She rolled her eyes. "Which is why you're calling me, isn't it? You need me to do you a favor, don't you?"

"You might call it a favor. I might call it sourcing you on a story that is sure to rock the city and forever change the political landscape in this country."

Allison stopped. "That's quite the claim, Senator."

"Have I piqued your interest yet?" he asked.

"Maybe. I'm leaving work right now. Want to buy me a drink downtown?"

Blunt sighed. "I don't know. People will see us

together. And as this town is known to do, it will talk. I'd rather not be linked to you on this one."

"That makes me think this is either really good or I don't want to touch this story with a ten-foot pole."

"I know you've got more Emmys and Peabody Awards than you can shake a stick at, but this one might put you in the Pulitzer category."

Allison's eyes widened. "Consider my interest officially piqued."

"I'm leaving a package on your doorstep that has all the details. It'll give you more than enough to tell a great story and start investigating yourself."

"Just so we're clear, I'm not going to commit to anything," she said.

"I understand."

"Good. I wouldn't want to give you the impression that I'm just going to do whatever you suggest, especially without plenty of fact checking and sourcing."

"I'd expect nothing less."

"Now, are you going to tell me who the politician in question is, or do I have to guess?"

"It's Wilson Wellington."

"Wellington? I didn't expect that," she said. "He's squeaky clean as far as politicians go. I mean, he did have that affair, but who hasn't had a good one in this town?"

"That seems terribly mild compared to what you're about to learn regarding Wellington's past."

"Perhaps you don't recall, but that story chewed up hours and hours of multiple news cycles when the truth came to light."

"I promise you, that scandal will be a footnote on his Wikipedia page by the time you expose the world to who that man really is."

Allison hustled down the steps and then walked toward her car in the parking garage as they continued their conversation. "I appreciate the call and the opportunity to break this story, but why now? I'm sure this isn't some recent revelation."

"It's probably not new to the people who covered it up, but it is to me."

"Don't be coy with me, Senator. You didn't just finish your glass of scotch—"

"Bourbon," he corrected.

"Sorry," she said with a chuckle as she climbed inside her vehicle. "Didn't mean to offend you. So you didn't just finish your glass of bourbon and decide to give me a call, did you? There's something else going on here, isn't there?"

Blunt paused for a moment before answering. "Should I leave this package with you or give it to someone else who wants to break the story of the year?"

"Fine," she said. "I'll take it. But just remember I'm not obligated to run it."

"If you actually read it and then don't, you'll be doing your viewers a disservice. America deserves to know what kind of man Wilson Wellington is."

"I guess you'll have to trust me to be the judge of that," Allison said. "Good night, Senator."

She hung up and exhaled. After a long day that included plenty of interoffice drama, she wanted to process what had happened. But that would have to wait. J.D. Blunt was about to drop a story in her lap that he promised would be the story of the year. While that claim was made often by tipsters on her caller hotline or through her website—and quickly dismissed—she was intrigued.

Wilson Wellington had grown to be one of the most powerful men on Capitol Hill. If Blunt's information checked out, the fallout could indeed be life changing for both her and Wellington. She pushed the ignition button, and her car roared to life. As she sped home, she considered all the possibilities and took a moment to disconnect from the grind of her day and dream. If she took down one of the most influential players in Washington, she would have a chance to become the city's most sought-after television personality when it came to news.

Allison was still lost in thought when she came

to a halt in front of her gated driveway. She waited as the gates swung open. The headlights from her car illuminated the yellow package leaning against her door that Blunt had left for her. She parked in the garage and hustled to pick up the files, anxious to read them.

She ripped open the top and dug out a handful of papers. Riveted by what she read, she immediately called one of her editors.

"Eric, I need you to help me check something out," she said.

He moaned. "Allison? Do you know what time it is?"

"Time for you to start looking into something for me."

"Okay, okay," he said. "What is it?"

"I got a hot tip about Wilson Wellington. He might have been involved in this big cover-up plot that resulted in the death of an American pilot."

"Text me some of the info, and I'll start looking into it."

"And hurry, Eric. This could be huge."

She hadn't moved, still flipping through the pages when her phone rang a few minutes later.

"Who's calling me now?" she asked aloud. She peered at the number on the screen but didn't recognize it.

"This is Allison," she said after she jammed her cell between her right shoulder and ear. She flipped a few pages, trying to scan them beneath the exterior porch light.

"Allison, this is Wilson Wellington."

She almost dropped the phone as his voice arrested her attention. "Senator Wellington, what a surprise. I don't usually get calls this late from anyone, much less someone like yourself."

"Well, please accept my apologies for the late time of this call, but I was at a private gathering this evening after dinner, and this is the first opportunity I've had to call you."

"You were at the Alibi Club, weren't you?"

Wellington laughed. "Now, Allison, you know that even if I was in that club—which I'm wasn't—I couldn't talk about that with you. No members are allowed to discuss their status with the public."

"Okay, Senator. I get it. You can't tell me. So, what do you need?"

"I need you to do me a favor and squash a story that's being circulated by J.D. Blunt. You haven't heard from him, have you?"

"Now, Senator, if you can't reveal your membership in the Alibi Club, I can't reveal my sources to any stories I may or may not be working on."

"This is why The Carter Connection is my favorite news program," Wellington said. "You're sharp and witty."

"I'm also impervious to flattery, so if you don't have anything else for me, it's been a long day."

"Actually, I have a story that I want to give you about the intelligence community. And in exchange, you must agree to kill those lies Blunt is pedaling and trying to pass off as the truth. Interested in striking some sort of agreement? As you may well know, I've got a very good opportunity to win my party's nomination and win the presidency."

"If I were working on a story, I might be willing to squash it for the next one. But that all depends on the story."

"Fair enough. If you hold off on anything Blunt gave you, I promise to deliver you a story that will undoubtedly win you truckloads of awards."

"I'll be waiting," she said before hanging up.

A wide grin spread across her face as she realized she couldn't lose. She'd obviously stumbled into something—and two of Capitol Hill's biggest power brokers had engaged her in their game.

And it was a game that she was going to win one way or another.

CHAPTER 19

TWO DAYS LATER, Blunt stumbled out of bed and headed straight for his study. He spent most of the night imagining how he was going to handle the subsequent fallout of Wilson Wellington being destroyed politically and what the cagey veteran of Capitol Hill might do to exact revenge. And while Blunt wanted to see the story appear almost instantaneously on websites across the country, he knew Allison Carter needed more time to reach out to different sources before publishing the story and the supporting documents.

Political Armageddon wasn't Blunt's preferred method to resolve issues. He tried to squelch Allan Elliott's hearing through more diplomatic means, giving Wellington a chance to respond in kind, but the olive branch had been met with an iron fist. Blunt was just thankful this wasn't the early nineteenth century, or else he would've likely been challenged to a duel.

After turning on his laptop, Blunt started a pot of coffee in the kitchen before returning to his desk. He navigated to his favorite news site and opened up the front page.

Nothing.

At least nothing Blunt hoped to see. The lead article was about oil leeching into a West Virginia river and sickening hundreds downstream from the incident. The next two stories detailed a struggling economy and how President Michaels intended to fix it as well as a primer on Elliott's scheduled hearing.

Blunt let out a string of expletives before stomping back to the kitchen. He snarled as he poured his coffee, grousing aloud about how Allison Carter's lack of expediency cost his credibility, at least in the eyes of Wilson Wellington. No longer could Blunt's threats be considered serious. He'd be perceived as a feckless has-been, still trying to maintain relevance in the nation's capital. Or as his father used to say, "Son, don't be all bark and no bite. Even if someone gets away, take a hunk of flesh from them."

His father's words weren't literal instructions, but they made Blunt smile, a moment of levity in an otherwise tense situation. He could still hear his father's baritone voice doling out the words of wisdom. But the meaning was clear: You may not take someone down, but let them remember you. Blunt figured that if he wanted to make a permanent mark on Wellington, one that wouldn't easily be scrubbed from the public's collective memory, he'd have to do some damage.

Blunt finished his coffee before dialing The Carter Connection host's number.

"This is Allison Carter," she said, her voice light and polished.

"I was afraid I might wake you up," Blunt said.

"Mister Blunt, what a pleasure it is to speak to you this morning. As you might know, this town likes to get a jump on the rest of the country. I can't just sit around all morning. There's plenty of work to be done."

"Speaking of which, I—"

"Stop right there, Mr. Blunt. I know why you're calling. The truth of the matter is I'm not ready to publish anything from the information you gave me."

"Was there a problem?"

"Well, I haven't finished all my research."

Blunt stood and paced around the room. "Is that the only thing that's holding you up?"

"At the moment, yes. However, there's also a hearing I need to cover today, a hearing that I believe you're expected to be at."

"That's a farce," he said. "Allan Elliott is barely old enough to be serving in Congress, let alone taking up a crusade to deconstruct our intelligence community through some damn witch hunt. I know it. You know it. The American people know it. This whole thing just reeks of political grandstanding."

"Everybody makes a name for themselves on Capitol Hill in different ways."

"It's certainly not the most prudent."

"Have you ever considered that perhaps Elliott isn't intent on becoming a career politician? He might have his eye on something else. And if he gets a reputation for dragging Washington's shadowy organizations into the light, he's liable to find plenty of opportunities."

"They might not be the kind of opportunities he wants."

"Maybe not to you, but the shrewdest people in this city are the ones who can pick their way through the minefield of partisan politics and reach the other side to find open arms. You're one of those people."

"My background dictated that I do what I do. Consultants for the Department of Defense are in short supply, especially ones with my background."

"Is that what you consider yourself? A consultant? You're more like a puppet master."

Blunt huffed a laugh through his nose. "I don't know who's telling you those lies, but that's what they are—lies. I give advice, which isn't always taken. Like with you. I give you everything you need to win a Pulitzer, and then you just walk away."

"I haven't said I'm not going to do anything with what you gave me. I just need more time."

"Burn me now, and you'll be playing with fire, Miss Carter."

"Well, this escalated quickly," she said. "I need to be going. I've got a hearing to get to."

"I'll see you there," Blunt said with a growl.

Blunt hung up and then called Besserman.

"What happened?" he asked as he answered. "I kept looking for a big report about Wellington's past sins in the military."

"Apparently, it's still being researched and fact checked, but I'm not buying it," Blunt said. "There was just something about Allison when I spoke with her this morning. She just seemed off."

"What do you mean?"

"It's like she was dodgy and trying to hide something. She gave me a lot of rehearsed answers just to try and satisfy my questions. But I only have more now, chiefly among them—what's really holding her back?"

"Think Wellington got to her?" Besserman asked.

"How could he have known what we were doing?"

"I would never discount his involvement in everything. He's one of the most well-connected people in all of Washington. All she had to do was make one phone call, and who knows who was listening."

"Geez, Bobby, you make Wellington sound like he has his own personal NSA."

"He might. There's no telling how many people at my agency might owe him favors or could be involved in helping him on one level or another."

"That's scary."

"Exactly—which is why we need to be careful when handling this issue. I don't think there's anything wrong with what you did, but you shouldn't be surprised if Wellington is the one who somehow managed to dissuade Allison Carter from pursuing that story."

"Then I'll go to someone else," Blunt said.

Besserman sighed. "You know it's going to be like that no matter where you go."

"What about one of those websites?"

"Those are even worse, aside from the fact that only fringe people read them. They're worse than tabloids go when it comes to credibility. If you want this story to gain traction, it needs to be someone like Allison Carter who looks directly into the camera and stakes her reputation on a report that Wilson

Wellington is guilty of war crimes and tried to cover it up."

Blunt stared at the chair in front of him, mulling over if he wanted to kick it over. After a split second, he realized he did want to smash his foot into it and send the chair flying across the room. But he also didn't want the accompanying pain. So, he relented.

"I need to get going," Blunt said. "I have to testify at that damn hearing."

"Don't worry, J.D.," Besserman said. "We'll think of something."

CHAPTER 20

CIA safe house
Undisclosed location in Virginia

ANTOINE KNELT AND TIED his shoes. He licked his thumb and tried to rub a scuff off the toe. With a little work, he managed to get the mark to budge, leaving both tips equally shiny. After taking a deep breath, he strode over to the window on the back of the door and studied his image before returning to the bed.

The CIA had moved him after Blunt paid a visit to a small mountain home somewhere outside of Washington. Antoine wasn't sure where it was, but he didn't care. He was close enough. If he needed to, he could find his way back to the city to take care of the unfinished business he had.

From his bedroom, he could hear one of the agents babysitting him talking on the phone. Several hours had passed since the other one uttered a word, leading Antoine to conclude that only one of them was in the room.

Antoine ventured around the corner and peered at Dax, the CIA agent assigned to watching the almost-assassin for the United States. The operative bolted upright from his more relaxed situation and studied Antoine closely.

"I don't know why you got all dressed up today," the agent said. "You're not going anywhere. Do you think you have a date?"

Antoine nodded. "A date with destiny."

The agent snickered and shook his head before walking into the kitchen and grabbing a plate containing eggs, bacon, and toast from the microwave. "So cooking is my hobby, and you're my captive customer."

Antoine crinkled his nose and drew back.

"Oh, come on," the agent said. "I didn't poison it. And most importantly, I didn't over salt it either. Just try it."

Antoine didn't budge.

"Your blood sugar level is going to plummet," the agent said, shoving the food toward his prisoner. "Take it for goodness' sake."

Antoine reached for the plate but pulled his hands back at the last moment, sending the breakfast crashing to the floor. The agent cursed several times and yelled at Antoine.

"Just get out of here, you ungrateful piece of garbage," the man said as he knelt to clean up the mess.

The commotion awoke the other operative, who scrambled out of his room and squinted before shielding his eyes from the light. "What the hell is going on out here? I'm trying to get some sleep in there you know."

The agent on the ground looked up. "We had a little mishap here with butterfingers. But he's going back to his room now. Isn't that right?"

Antoine shook his head. "I don't think so."

Both operatives froze, eyeing Antoine carefully.

The guard on the floor stood and neared his captive. "Perhaps I need to rephrase that: Go to your room."

"I'm fine right here. Thank you," Antoine said before winking at the man.

"That's not very smart, my friend," the agent said. "I have orders to keep you safe and not to harm you. But maybe those orders got misplaced somewhere. Now where were they?"

The agent looked around for a few seconds before scooping up a group of documents. He crammed them into a blender on the kitchen counter. With the flip of a switch, the appliance sputtered before whirring smoothly and shredding the paper.

"Oops," the agent said. "Looks like they're gone."

Antoine glared at the man. "Do you think that's supposed to scare me?"

"Maybe this will," he said, removing his pistol from its holster.

Antoine smirked before collapsing to the floor.

"Damn it," the other agent said. "Didn't you read that bit about him being a diabetic in his file? I bet you didn't even feed him."

"Why do you think this food was everywhere? This idiot dropped the plate I was trying to give him."

Antoine kept his eyes closed as he eased his finger over his blood sugar monitor. He pressed a button, resulting in the emission of an ultrasonic sound. Thanks to the plugs he'd secured in his ears before exiting his room, the noise had no effect on him. The same couldn't be said for the two agents.

After waiting for a pair of thuds, Antoine climbed to his feet and then smiled as he surveyed the aftermath of his stunt. He removed one of the agent's blazers and tried it on. Satisfied with the fit, Antoine proceeded to tie both men up. He fished the keys to the SUV out of their pants and pocketed both their phones.

The next order of business involved moving both of his former captors into the back of the vehicle. Utilizing a wheelbarrow found in the back, Antoine hoisted each agent inside and steered them to the tailgate, where he schlepped the men inside. He gagged them and secured their hands to hooks so they couldn't get free.

Antoine drove a mile down the road before he chucked the cells out the window and into the woods encroaching the road. He ran his fingers through his hair before leaning his head back and laughing. While he hadn't been captive that long, freedom felt great.

He couldn't wait to get to the next phase of his plan.

CHAPTER 21

BLACK AWOKE EARLY, unable to get a restful night of sleep. Until about 2:30 a.m., he stared at the ceiling in the dark, contemplating every type of accusation that Antoine had leveled against J.D. Blunt. And after mulling over all the different scenarios as to why Blunt might be directing an LLC with ties to the Russian arms dealer Andrei Orlovsky, Black decided to go straight to the source. When Antoine initially made those claims about Blunt, Black wanted to dismiss them as bluster from a jilted operative. But Black's search led him back to Antoine, who acted as if he had intimate knowledge of Blunt's business dealings with Blue Moon Rising.

Black called in a favor with Mallory Kauffman to see if she could locate the exact safe house where the CIA was holding Antoine. She groused about being woken up so early, but she owed Black several favors, especially after he handled one of her stalker ex-boyfriends.

"You do realize it's not even six o'clock?" she asked after he explained what he wanted.

"I know," Black said. "This isn't something I plan to make a habit out of."

"It better not be," she said.

Mallory then went on to explain that moving Antoine from the black site in such a short amount of time seemed somewhat odd.

"How so?" Black asked.

"Well, that's certainly not standard protocol," she said. "You don't end up at a black site unless they have good reason to keep you there. But to transfer him so soon to a much lower-level facility? I mean, a safe house? That's like going from a prison to a detention hall."

"What would make the agency move him?"

She shrugged. "There are plenty of reasons why they might move him, though none of them make much sense in his case."

"Such as?"

"Antoine has diabetes, though that would get a transfer to a CIA-affiliated hospital," she said. "Or he could have a mental condition. Or maybe they had a higher priority prisoner transferring in. They like to keep those places occupied by only one mastermind fugitive at a time."

"But you haven't heard anything that would fit the bill for that?"

She shook her head. "Like I said, it's mind boggling. No one else is at the site. And if he had some health issues, surely he would be at a hospital by now."

"But he's not?" Black asked.

"Nope. You'll find him near a little town called Sperryville just outside one of Shenandoah National Park's entrances. It's about an hour and half from Washington, maybe even sooner at this time in the morning."

"Text me the directions," Black said. "I'm already heading out the door."

"You got it," Mallory said. "I would tell you that you owe me one, but I think I still owe you."

"I'm not keeping count," he said. "This is a huge help."

"Good luck," she said before ending their call.

Black hustled to his car and began the trek toward Sperryville. As he drove, he mulled over what he would ask Antoine. As a potential agent who failed to make the cut, he might say anything to cast Blunt in a bad light. The questions needed to extract the kind of information that would be easily proven when scrutinized. Black wasn't going to fall for a smokescreen from Antoine.

While the trip took longer than Black would've liked, he enjoyed the solitude. Leaving Washington at this time of morning meant passing a steady stream of headlights from commuters making their way into the city. Black's lanes, however, were virtually empty.

By the time he reached the edge of Shenandoah National Park, the sun had started to rise. Frost still coated the leaves, both fallen and clinging to their tree, all colorful in all their late-autumn glory. He followed the instructions Mallory had given and turned onto an unlined road, just wide enough for two vehicles to pass one another. Clocking his odometer, he slowed his vehicle as he approached the 1.4-mile marker and looked for the dirt driveway. He spotted the mailbox and eased up the hill leading to the house, which was barely visible through the dense woods comprised primarily of oak and pine trees.

After Black parked, he placed his right hand on his pistol and opened the door with his left. He had been to dozens of safe houses over the years, yet he couldn't remember going to one without a car present on the premises. He knocked on the door and waited.

When no one answered, he checked the doorknob and eased inside.

"Hello? Is anyone here?" Black called.

No reply.

Methodically moving from one room to the next, Black cleared the house. He considered the possibility that maybe there was a basement but couldn't find any access. After sweeping the area, he went into the kitchen and tried to survey the situation. He glanced down and noticed some scrambled eggs on the floor and the house in disarray. If agents suddenly moved Antoine, they did so in a hurry. Plates, silverware, and glasses were strewn across the counter, and all the beds remained unmade.

Black dialed Mallory's number again, hoping she might be able to provide an explanation for the vacancy at the safe house.

"No one's there?" she asked.

"Not a soul. Was there a transfer?"

"Hang on a second," she said, her keyboard clicking in the background. "There's nothing in the system about Antoine being switched to another location."

"And the place is a wreck," Black said as he walked through the house again. "Wherever they went, it certainly appears like they left in a rush."

"Let me look in one more place," she said. After a brief pause. "Nope, nothing there either. I've got no idea what happened, but it's alarming. Is there anything I can do?"

"I would tell you to let someone at the agency know, but then you'd be outed for giving out the address to one of their safe houses."

"Yeah, my hands are tied there."

"I understand," he said. "I'll think of something."

Black hung up and immediately called Blunt to let him know that Antoine might be on the loose.

"Please answer," Black said after the fourth ring.

Then the call went to voicemail.

Black left a message warning Blunt of the possible situation with Antoine. Then, Black rushed back to his car and returned to Washington.

He called Shields to update her on the situation.

"Have you seen Blunt this morning?" he asked.

"Not yet. He should've been in by now. Why? What's wrong?"

"I just drove out to the CIA safe house where the agency was keeping Antoine—"

"You did what?"

"I'll explain later, but Antoine is gone."

"Gone? What do you mean gone?" she asked.

"He wasn't there, and neither were any of the agents guarding him. And I can't find out any info about his whereabouts."

"Did you think you'd just place a call to the CIA switchboard and get a location for him?"

Black pounded the steering wheel as he got stuck behind a cement truck poking along the winding two-lane road.

"I spoke with Mallory Kauffman, but she doesn't know anything more," he said.

"More?"

"Who do you think got me the location of the safe house in the first place?"

"What are you doing?" she asked, her voice climbing an octave with each word. "People are going to learn that you're very much alive real soon if you keep this up."

"I know, I know. But if Blunt is involved in something nefarious, I can't just turn a blind eye."

"I get that, but do you realize everything that you're putting at risk by doing this?"

Black cocked his head to the side in an attempt to peer around the truck holding him up. "I'm aware of the consequences if I get caught, just as I'm aware of what might happen if we later find out that we're working for a megalomaniac who's using us to further some personal agenda."

"Or maybe it's not personal," she said. "Look, I get where you're coming from. Trust is in short supply in this shadowy world of ours. But we both know Blunt. Does he strike you as the kind of person who'd be running some devious scheme behind closed doors? He sure doesn't to me."

"That's why the best agents never get caught without some stroke of luck," Black said as he roared around the truck and floored the accelerator. "He could have the wool pulled squarely over our eyes, and we'd never be the wiser."

"Blunt just wants good to prevail. And he'd rather err on the side of exposing the truth for what the fallout would mean for the good of this country. He's going to tell the truth no matter what, which is why he isn't so well-liked in Washington."

"You're absolutely right," Black said. "That's why there's only one place Antoine could be."

Black hung up and narrowed his eyes as he merged onto the interstate.

CHAPTER 22

Washington, D.C.

ANTOINE SLUNG A BAG over his shoulder as he trudged up the steps to the Capitol Building. He nodded and smiled at the guard directing everyone through the metal detectors. One guy sporting an Armani suit and slicked-back hair complained about having to take off his belt loud enough for everyone within a hundred-foot radius to hear. He snarled at the woman operating the conveyor belt and made a snide comment about placing Italian leather on a germ-infested machine.

"There's one in every crowd," the man in front of Antoine said.

"Just one?" Antoine cracked.

The man chuckled. "Around here, there's at least four or five."

Not even ten seconds later, a woman clad in a white pants suit raised her hands in the air and stamped her foot.

"Don't you know who I am?" she asked. "If I let you run this through that machine of yours, it might get dirty. And let me assure you that my editors won't be happy if I have a dirty jacket for my report."

"Lady, nobody watches your show anyway," the security guard said.

"Tell that to the millions who tune in each night to watch what I have to say about the happenings here in our nation's capital."

"Fake news," the guard quipped. "Now move along or you're going to have millions upset that you're holding up the line."

She glared at him, which he laughed off as he ushered her through the metal detector.

"See what I mean," the man in front of Antoine said. "It's a zoo in here. I'm just shocked that woman didn't have a legion of bare-chested man slaves carry her here on a howdah."

Antoine raised his eyebrows. "Far too many entitled people around here literally getting away with murder."

"Ain't that the truth," the man said.

Antoine flung his bag onto the X-ray machine belt and moved through the line as instructed.

"Do you have anything metal in your pockets?" a guard asked him.

Antoine shook his head. "I do have my blood sugar monitor."

The guard held out a small dish and waited for Antoine to remove the medical device. Once he complied, he was ushered into the metal detector. After he was cleared, he gathered his belongings and asked a congressional page to point him to where the Elliott hearings were taking place.

Antoine followed the directions, meandering down the hall. He walked slowly, eyeing the number of armed guards patrolling the main corridor. After pacing back and forth, he waited until he saw one of the security team members slip into the men's restroom. Antoine followed and selected a stall right next to the man.

While the man was washing his hands, Antoine seized his opportunity, inserting his ear plugs before activating the ultrasonic device. Seconds later, the man collapsed in a heap as did the few people occupying the stalls. Antoine dragged the officer into one of the stalls and propped him up on the toilet before snagging the man's pistol.

Antoine made his way toward the hearing room, smiling politely at the guards strolling through the hall. He found a dark-haired page and bumped into him to snag his identification badge off his lapel. The young man's picture was emblazoned on the card, but the small, grainy image likely wouldn't be scrutinized by the guard at the door. And Antoine was right, getting waved inside after a quick peek at the picture.

Antoine pocketed the badge and ambled over to the media members clustered together. He took a seat next to the reporter who'd made a fuss in the security line.

"Are we going to get anything good out of this?" Antoine asked the woman.

She gave him a sideways glance. "Who are you with?"

"The Drudge Report," he said. "And you?"

She rolled her eyes. "The fact that they allow bloggers to sit with the media corps shows that just about anyone can be considered a member of the media these days."

"I'm sorry," Antoine said. "I didn't catch your name again."

She slowly turned to him and glared. "Are times so hard at your little website that they can't pay you enough to afford a television?"

"Oh, that's right," Antoine said. "I recognize you now. It's just that you look completely different in person than you do on camera after they've covered you up with all that makeup."

"My, aren't you a charmer," she said as she rolled her eyes.

"I'm not here to make friends. I'm here for the truth."

"Good luck getting it out of these fellas. They trade in lies. I doubt we'll hear one true thing the entire time we're in this room today."

Antoine eyed her closely. "I wouldn't be so sure."

"Do you know something the rest of us don't?"

He shook his head. "I just have a feeling."

A hush fell over the room as several committee members marched up to their seats at the front of the room. Chairman Ian Henry was the last to ease into his chair before calling the meeting into order.

For the next five minutes, he outlined the rules for the interview period, explaining how much time each member had for their respective questions for the different witnesses subpoenaed for the hearing. When he was finished, he looked at the member on the far end of the row and nodded.

"For my first witness, I'd like to call Special Consultant to the Department of Defense, former Senator J.D. Blunt," the man said.

This ought to be good.

Antoine pulled his bag onto his lap and reached inside, wrapping his hand around the gun and then fingering the trigger. He couldn't wait to watch Blunt squirm—and then die.

CHAPTER 23

BLUNT GRABBED THE seat back in front of him and pulled himself to his feet when he was called as the first witness by Arizona Congressman Albert Zuckerman. When Blunt represented Texas as a senator, he made an enemy out of Zuckerman by squashing one of his bills when it came to the floor. He didn't even try to disguise the Zuckerman-Harding Act, which was touted as an answer to prop up the flagging social security system but was actually a wide-ranging piece of legislation stuffed full of pork. If the portion of the law that drew all the attention was passed, tax payers would've footed a modest bill. But as it was written, the cost quadrupled after factoring in all the handouts for the various districts set to reap a windfall.

When Blunt served as an elected official, he took the position entrusted to him by his constituents seriously and saw the passage of such a piece of legislation to be morally reprehensible. So, he used procedural rules to keep it from ever even seeing the light of day in the Senate. And for that, Zuckerman vowed to get revenge on Blunt one day.

That day had finally arrived.

As the chairman reminded Blunt that he was under oath, he sat down.

"Welcome, Senator Blunt," Zuckerman said, a faint smile appearing at the corners of his mouth. "We appreciate your willingness to come before this committee in an effort to shed some light on how the U.S. conducts itself abroad and at home as it pertains to our intelligence gathering."

"It's really simple," Blunt said. "We act within the confines of the law."

"In that case, would you mind walking us through how you gather information on American citizens?"

Blunt furrowed his brow as he leaned forward to speak into his mic. "I'm sure you know that we aren't allowed to gather information on our own citizens, right?"

"Of course you are," Zuckerman said. "And you aren't leaving that stand until you explain the means and method by which you've been operating."

"I'm afraid you don't understand what I do," Blunt said.

Zuckerman leaned back in his chair and interlocked his fingers, resting them on his bulging belly. "Enlighten us then."

"I consult with the Department of Defense on matters of national security."

"And what makes you qualified to handle this?"

"You'd have to ask the men who hired me. They're the ones who feel I'm well-suited for my position."

Zuckerman shrugged. "In that case, humor us."

Blunt sighed. "Aside from serving on the foreign relations and intelligence committees, I have a background in intelligence while serving during the conflict in Vietnam. Prior to getting elected to public office, I served briefly with the CIA."

"And while you were a member of the CIA, did you ever spy on anyone illegally?"

Blunt scowled. "Excuse me, Mr. Chairman, I didn't realize I was on trial here."

Henry glared at Zuckerman. "Can we please keep the line of questioning within the parameters that we established prior to holding this hearing?"

"Of course, sir," Zuckerman said before returning his gaze to Blunt. "Now, let me rephrase that question: Did you ever witness any illegal information gathering practices conducted by the CIA during your time there?"

Blunt sighed. "That was a long time ago, but off the top of my head, I don't believe I recall any instance where we broke the law to spy on our own citizens. If we ever did anything that came close to crossing the line, it was always in the best interest of our citizens and protecting them from danger. But I don't recollect any specific instance."

"But there were times when that happened?"

"Maybe. Like I said, there are times when you just need to get the data to make an informed decision. And there are moments where we might need to bend the rules a little. But there's a group of judges who oversee this activity to ensure that we stay above board in everything we do. The law is there to protect its citizens, but so are we."

"So you're saying that when these two things are in conflict with one another, we should just trust that people are going to do the right thing?"

Blunt nodded. "The agency wasn't—nor is it—full of evil people. And neither is the military. You'll always find a bad apple or two floating around. But in general, people are respectful of the laws governing this great country and do their best to work within them."

"It's funny that you should use that phrase there: do their best," Zuckerman said. "I know you're very careful with your words, especially since you're under oath. But that's an interesting way to say that you don't always comply with the law."

"In keeping our nation safe, operatives in every intelligence agency sometimes find themselves in gray areas in the moment," Blunt said. "But there's no willful lawbreaking that I've ever witnessed."

"Never?"

Blunt shrugged. "If there is, I haven't seen it."

"So you're saying everyone is squeaky clean?"

"Do you drive yourself to and from work every day, Mr. Congressman?" Blunt asked.

Zuckerman withdrew and scowled before replying slowly. "Yes, but I don't see what that has to do with—"

"Do you ever drive above the speed limit?" Blunt pressed.

"I try to use my cruise control and stay within the prescribed limits."

"So you never speed?"

Zuckerman shook his finger at Blunt. "I know where you're going with this and—"

"From your answer, it's easy to conclude that you sometimes exceed the limits, am I right?"

"But I—"

"Despite your occasional misdeeds behind the wheel, I doubt you would characterize yourself as a reckless driver since your record shows that you haven't received a ticket since moving to the capital. Now, I don't know if that's a result of professional courtesy from Metro police or if you're really cautious. But, today, you're on record as saying that you do your best but implied that you don't always adhere to the letter of the law. However, nobody is worried you're going to go flying around the Beltway tomorrow and hit four cars and cause a major pileup. Likewise, you shouldn't be concerned about the status of our intelligence community. They're doing their best to make sure you can sleep at night without worrying about getting blown up by terrorists."

A partisan applause erupted. Zuckerman threw up his hands in a gesture to quiet the attendees.

"Settle down," Chairman Henry said. "This isn't about scoring political points. This is about finding out how our intelligence agencies comply with the law."

"Thank you," Zuckerman said, his nostrils flaring.

"Unfortunately, that's all the time allotted to you," the chairman said.

"But I'm not done," Zuckerman protested. "The witness's long-winded answers ate up all my time."

Henry shrugged. "You should've known you were dealing with a former politician."

Blunt shot a glance at Zuckerman, winking before leaking a wry smile.

"Congressman Elliott, your five minutes begins now," Henry said.

Elliott nodded at Henry. "Thank you, Mr. Chairman. And now that I'm well versed with Mr. Blunt's tactics, perhaps we'll get some real answers out of him."

"I have nothing to hide," Blunt said.

"Excellent," Elliott said. "Then let's begin with my first question. As I was reviewing some of the budgets, I noticed that you're listed as a consultant in connection with seventy-five million in discretionary funds. Mr. Blunt, what exactly do you do?"

"I help advise the Department of Defense regarding certain policy decisions," Blunt said.

"And what exactly does that look like?"

"I share my opinion about the best way forward to maneuver through the turbulent waters of Middle Eastern diplomacy," Blunt said. "It's not too complicated."

"Is that all you do?"

"In a manner of speaking, yes."

"Are you sure you don't want to amend your answer, Mr. Blunt? Or do I need to remind you that you're currently under oath?"

Blunt swallowed hard as he eyed his hard-charging interrogator.

A hush fell over the crowd as it anxiously awaited Blunt's response.

CHAPTER 24

BLACK GROWLED AS HE STARED at the gridlock in front of him. He tuned the radio to a news station in an attempt to find out if there was anything causing the blockage or just another routine day in rush hour traffic. After five minutes of no movement, he picked up his phone to search for an app that would help him plot the fastest route to the Capitol Building through the current logjam.

As soon as the flow resumed, he took the next off-ramp and weaved his way through surface streets. When he came to a stoplight, he called Shields to update her on his status.

"How far away are you?" she asked.

"Maybe fifteen minutes until I get parked," he said. "Were you able to reach Blunt yet?"

"Nothing."

"Keep trying. We've got to get him out of there because he'll be a sitting duck for Antoine."

"You think he's going to try something in a public place?" Shields asked.

"Without a doubt. He's got a vendetta against Blunt and wants public retribution. The only question is when he's going to do it."

"Well, Blunt has just been called forward as the first person to be questioned to kick off the hearing."

Black let out a string of expletives. "And I can't do a thing about it stuck here in traffic. If I hadn't gone to that safe house this morning . . ."

"If you hadn't gone, you wouldn't be alarmed. You wouldn't even be going to the hearing, so stay focused. We'll still have a chance to stop Antoine."

"Can you hack into the Capitol Building and set off the fire alarm?" Black asked. "I mean, anything to get Blunt out of there and buy me some more time."

"That'd take too long. Besides, a fire alarm would create mass chaos and be easier for Antoine to do something to Blunt."

Black sighed. "You're right. Can you at least leave an anonymous tip with Capitol Hill police that there's an assassin sitting in that hearing?"

"I'll do my best. Remember to call me when you get there."

"Roger that."

"And, Black?"

"Yeah?"

"I know you're going to be in a rush when you arrive, but don't forget to put your coms in so we can stay in touch."

"Of course."

"Be safe."

Black turned to the right to find a stretch of light traffic and reached the parking near the Capitol Building five minutes earlier than expected. He jammed the coms into his ear, grabbed a baseball cap and a pair of sunglasses, and took off running.

CHAPTER 25

BLUNT TOOK A SIP of water, anything to stall responding. He hoped that one of the congressmen on the panel, fellow lawmakers that he considered to be his friends, would come to his rescue. But they all remained silent, awaiting Blunt's answer.

"We're all waiting," Elliott said. "Take your time. I don't want you to perjure yourself."

Blunt sighed before he began. "I'm afraid there's not much more to say. You're on some fishing expedition, perhaps at the behest of your constituents. But all of my work with the D.O.D. is sanctioned, lawful, and effective at keeping you and all of the American people safe from attacks on this country as well as protecting our interests abroad."

"That's a mighty evasive answer," Elliott said. "And not what I asked. Now, let me repeat this again. Aside from advising the D.O.D., is that all you do?"

"That's a broad description of what I do, so I

guess I'm not sure exactly what you're after."

"Let me rephrase the question: How can you justify a budget line item that large if all you do is consult?"

"I'm not the comptroller," Blunt said. "You'll have to ask him."

"Do you think what you do justifies a budget this substantial?"

Blunt shifted in his seat before answering. "I know that you're new to Capitol Hill, so perhaps you should've discussed this with some of your peers who understand how all this works. The finance committee approves the D.O.D.'s budget. If you don't like how the country's money is being spent, there are other avenues to address this. Having a hearing isn't going to fix this."

"I'm trying to understand the waste Washington dumps on the nation's taxpayers each year, but thank you for the civics lesson. I know how this works."

Blunt's eyebrows shot upward, and he cocked his head to one side. "Are you sure about that? Because these questions you're asking are ones that could easily be answered by members of the finance committee. For someone who's worried so much about waste, you're wasting the government's resources as well as plenty of people's time."

Chairman Henry butted in. "If you don't have

any other line of questioning, Mr. Elliott, I suggest you cede your remaining time to another congressman."

Elliott shuffled the papers in front of him and peered over the top of his glasses at Henry. "I'm not even close to being done."

"Then, please, get on with it," Henry said.

Elliott straightened his tie and continued. "This is a very straightforward question. What role did you play in the death of Guy Hirschbeck?"

"Whoa, whoa, whoa," Blunt said as he snarled at Elliott. "This was billed as a hearing about transparency regarding the D.O.D., not an opportunity for partisan politicians to fling around scurrilous accusations without any basis. Please, Mr. Chairman, address this clown show or I'm going to show you how to filibuster a hearing. This is insane."

Henry held his hands up in the air. "Everyone, please settle—"

"Based on your answer, I'm going to assume a big role," Elliott said as he leaned forward and spoke into his mic, drowning out the chairman.

"For the record, Mr. Freshman Congressman, I was saddened to hear about Senator Hirschbeck's unfortunate murder. We often faced off on different sides of issues, but we were still cordial toward one another."

"Intentionally screwing up his last name is cordial? Good to know."

A murmur spread across the court.

"I don't know what political website you've been ingesting as if it's the truth, but you need to simmer down because you don't know what you're talking about."

"So, you didn't direct anyone to kill Senator Hirschbeck, even though he threatened to expose your secret organization?"

"You have quite the fanciful imagination, Mr. Elliott. In Texas, we have a saying: Always drink upstream from the herd. These questions are so ridiculous I'm starting to think you're the kind of guy who'd drink downstream."

Elliott glared at Blunt. "You didn't answer my question."

Blunt leaned up to the mic and pursed his lips. "Listen very closely. No."

A man from the audience stood and pointed at Blunt, shouting. "Liar! Liar!"

CHAPTER 26

BLACK PUMPED HIS ARMS as he raced across the lawn toward the steps of the Capitol Building. Tour groups and congressional personnel milled around the entrance, unconcerned with a single man sprinting full speed toward the doors. Black's lungs burned as he couldn't get his legs to move fast enough to his liking. He flashed the CIA badge he'd been issued at the security guard before jumping ahead in line and scooting thought the metal detector without setting off any alarms.

"Are you still with me?" Black asked Shields over the coms.

"I'm not going anywhere," she said. "Just tell me what you need."

"What's happening with the proceedings?"

"It's getting testy in there," she said. "Elliott is really going after Blunt and throwing all kinds of accusations at him. Better hurry."

"Any sign of Antoine yet?"

"Not yet, but I'm watching this on C-SPAN. It's one stationary camera on the witness stand and the other is on the panel. There could be a thousand or two people in the room, and I wouldn't be able to tell the difference."

"Okay, I'm almost there."

While Black didn't want to draw unwanted attention for racing through the hallowed halls of Congress, this wasn't the moment to be worried about decorum. He flew past a pair of policeman and motioned for them to join him.

"What's the matter, sir?" one of the officers asked.

"We've got a situation at the hearing," Black shouted over his shoulder. "Please hurry."

The two men immediately followed Black and radioed in that there was a developing situation at the Elliott hearing.

"Get moving," Shields said over the coms. "It just got tense in there. I can't see who, but somebody is shouting, and it sounds like Antoine."

"I'm almost there," Black said. "And I've wrangled some Capitol Hill police too."

"I'll let you know if anything changes," she said.

Black rounded the corner and charged toward the door. Shouting spilled into the hallway, and he recognized Antoine's voice right away.

"Liar! Liar!" Antoine said.

Black put his hands in the air. "I apologize, Mr. Chairman, this is my uncle, and I just found out that he was off his meds. Please forgive us."

Antoine turned his gaze toward Black and narrowed his eyes. "Another lie. This man isn't my nephew, and I'm not on any meds. But I am on a crusade to make sure people know the truth about who that man really is."

Antoine pointed back at Blunt and approached the witness stand.

At that moment, the two police officers rushed into the room. Black directed them toward Antoine, and they rushed toward him.

Antoine noticed them and waved them off. "No, no. This is democracy in action—and justice, too."

He plunged his hand into his bag, prompting screams as people dove to the floor.

"He's got a gun!" one woman yelled.

Black noticed both officers go for their firearms when a strange thing happened. Everyone in the room with the exception of himself and Antoine collapsed to the ground in a heap.

Black stared slack-jawed at the scene. "What just happened?"

"You shouldn't be worried about what just happened. It's what's about to happen that should interest you the most."

Antoine pulled out the gun he'd lifted from the officer and shot out both cameras.

"What's going on in there?" Shields squawked. "I just saw the few people in view collapse, and I still can't see you or Antoine."

"I'll explain later," Black said. "Just call for help."

Black dove to the ground and snatched an officer's gun from its holster. Without hesitating, he fired at Antoine as he crept toward Blunt.

"Not today," Black said, firing at Antoine.

The jilted agent dove to the ground, avoiding several rounds. Both men took up positions behind tables. Black flipped one over and crouched low.

"You're never going to get out of here alive," Black said.

"You think I care about that? I came here to get justice and make sure the world learned what kind of man J.D. Blunt really is."

"You've guaranteed that whatever does happen, you won't be around to see it."

Moments later, two other Capitol Hill police officers stormed in the room.

Black shouted at them to get down, fearing that Antoine would shoot them. But he didn't. Instead, the two officers suddenly crumpled to the ground.

"What's going on in there?" Shields asked.

"It's kind of hard to explain, but everyone just keeps passing out. And I have no idea how he's doing it," Black said.

"How come you haven't collapsed?" she asked.

"I have no idea about that either. But thankfully he still has me to contend with or Blunt might already be dead."

Black peered around the edge of the overturned desk. "Where's Dr. Matthews? I know you didn't invent some device that could do this without him."

"Go to hell," Antoine said before he jumped to his feet and raced toward Blunt's limp body in the witness stand.

Black stood and took aim, squeezing off a couple rounds at Antoine. The first one hit him in the shoulder before he ducked, causing the second shot to miss. Antoine remained equidistant to Blunt as Black.

"Come on out," Black said, dragging the table with him as a shield while he moved toward his boss. "It's over."

"I'll be back," Antoine said. He fired two shots at Black before darting out one of the side doors and into the hallway. Black heard shouting from a security guard before silence.

Hustling into the hallway, Black found everyone in the vicinity lying on the ground, motionless.

But Antoine was gone.

CHAPTER 27

ANTOINE ACTIVATED THE ULTRASONIC device once he hit the hallway to clear the way. He raced toward the nearest restroom and sized up a man washing his hands before turning on the machine again. When the man fell to the floor, Antoine quickly undressed the man who'd been wearing a fedora and glasses. Law enforcement rushed back and forth in an effort to find Antoine. But he was intent on walking out of the Capitol Building like nothing ever happened.

After the hallways were relatively clear, he strode out and feigned shock as he noticed all the people lying on the floor. He hustled over to one of the security guards and inquired about what had just occurred, both to find out what they knew as well as to act like any normal concerned citizen would.

"What's going on?" Antoine asked.

"There was a disturbance at one of the hearings,"

the officer said. "We're looking for a man wearing a gray suit. There were reports of shots fired, but we haven't verified any of that yet. Just be careful out there."

"Of course," Antoine said as he nodded at the man and sauntered down the steps and toward the Federal Center station just a couple blocks away.

While in the bathroom, Antoine had siphoned a few twenty dollar bills out of the man's wallet. It wasn't much, but Antoine figured it would get him some food and a rail pass to get around the city until he figured out what he was going to do next. The element of surprise was now gone, so Blunt would be expecting an attack. However, the most troubling part of his plan was the fact that Titus Black was immune to the ultrasonic mechanism.

In all the testing Antoine had done before utilizing the device, not a single person had ever been able to withstand the frequency, knocking out everyone in a close vicinity for a minimum of five minutes. But not Black. He didn't even exhibit the slightest symptoms that the ultrasonic sound had on everyone else when the waves were emitted. The rest of the people in the hearing slumped to the floor in a matter of seconds. The operation should've been a smooth one. Call out Blunt for his hypocrisy, expose him as a fraud, then exact revenge for what he did.

Had Antoine's plan worked, he figured it would've been one helluva way to serve justice on Blunt.

But with the plot foiled, Antoine wasn't going to give up just yet. Blunt still needed to pay for what he did. Successfully pinning Senator Hirschbeck's murder on Blunt would be more challenging for sure but not impossible. Plenty of people in Washington wanted the former Texas senator out of the city all together. His trouble-making ways had come to a head, and something had to give.

Antoine stepped into the subway train that had just opened its doors. He didn't care where it was going. Until he assessed the situation and cobbled together a plan that could get revenge for what Blunt had done, Antoine was happy to ride anywhere and for as long as it took.

Blunt was going down, that much Antoine was sure of.

CHAPTER 28

BLUNT GRABBED HIS HEAD and grimaced as he pushed himself off the floor. All around the room, groans emanated from both the congressmen and the people on hand to witness the situation. With a furrowed brow, Blunt tried to determine what had happened. He closed his eyes, squeezing them shut as he hoped the pain would dissipate. But a couple minutes after regaining consciousness, he still felt like someone had walloped him over the head with a hammer.

"I move to adjourn this hearing," Chairman Henry said, his voice quivering as he spoke. "The committee will reassess and determine if this is truly necessary."

Blunt exhaled, counting the pain worth it all of a sudden. After Elliott's dismal performance, the majority of the committee members would likely vote against continuing the hearing. The optics were bad enough as Elliott appeared to be conducting little more than a personal witch hunt. Throw in the strange attack that left everyone in the room stunned and rendered incapacitated for a few minutes, and this was one event most sane representatives wouldn't want returning to Capitol Hill any time soon.

Wait.

The attack caused everyone in the room to lose consciousness—everyone except for Antoine.

And Black. Where's Titus Black? And how did he not get affected by all this?

Aside from wondering what the device was that Antoine used, Blunt also questioned why he was still alive. It had to be something to do with Black.

Black had burst into the hearing just as Antoine was about to take the lectern and deliver a screed unveiling all the sins he believed Blunt committed both past and present. But Antoine hadn't succeeded. And from what Blunt could tell, Antoine had escaped—but so had Black. Blunt fished his phone out of his pocket and prepared to dial Black's number when Chairman Henry approached.

"J.D., I'm really sorry about all this," he began. "What happened here today—"

"I don't need your apology," Blunt said. "Just squash this hearing from happening again, okay? This has probably already done far more harm than good."

"This is not what Elliott pitched to us when he said he wanted to conduct this hearing. The scope was much more limited, restricted to questions about the budget."

"This was an ambush," Blunt said. "It's not good for me. It's not good for the country. People don't want to know how the sausage is made. They just want to know that they won't ever have to witness planes flying into buildings and seeing iconic American structures on fire from flames stoked by terrorists—foreign or domestic."

"I know. It's just that we received a lot of pressure from Wilson Wellington and—"

"That's a man you ought to distance yourself from right there," Blunt said, pointing at Henry's chest. "Wellington has some skeletons that just might walk out of the closet real soon."

"He's difficult to avoid with all his pull around here."

"Trust me. You'll thank me later."

Someone tapped Blunt on the shoulder. He turned around and had a microphone thrust into his face.

"Mr. Blunt is the one you need to watch out for," Allison Carter said, nodding at Henry. "This is all just a deflection to keep you from finding out what he's up to."

Blunt forced a smile. "Ms. Carter, what a pleasant surprise. I offered you the story of a lifetime, but you turned it down. When the full story about Wellington breaks and your channel is playing catch up, I'm sure your editors will find it interesting that you declined to pursue the story of year."

She cocked her head to the side and smiled wryly. "No, you're going to be the story of the year. Americans everywhere are going to be demanding to know what your secret organization is doing and how you've been allowed to operate above the law for so long."

Blunt glared at her. "I don't know what you've been told, but I can assure you that it's all lies. I'm merely a consultant for the D.O.D. If you start trying to dig, you'll find a big fat dead end. Meanwhile, your competitor will be cleaning up in the ratings when they break the truth about Wellington."

"Are you threatening me, J.D., right here in front of Chairman Henry?" she asked.

He shook his head. "I'm merely warning you about the professional disgrace that will befall you if you don't focus your energy on the real criminal on Capitol Hill."

Allison kept her microphone near his mouth. "So, you're not willing to comment on Mr. Elliott's accusations?"

"You have two other stories that will be far more important to the American people than some manufactured exposé on how you think our national security should operate," Blunt said. "We keep

Americans like you safe and out of harm's way, but you think badgering me about this issue is going to result in more viewers? Good luck selling that story to the public."

"Thank you for your time," she said. "I have more than enough for a riveting story."

Blunt turned his focus back toward Henry. "This right here is why Elliott's hearing was a disaster. Don't let this happen again."

"What did happen here?" Henry asked. "One minute we were all watching some lunatic attack you, the next minute, we're waking up from what felt like a month-long slumber."

"I have no idea, but I intend to find out," Blunt said before spinning on his heels and striding toward the door.

Blunt was stopped at the door by a couple of Capitol Hill police. They wanted to interview him about what went down.

"There are a hundred other people in there who will tell you the same thing," Blunt said. "We don't know happened, just that we were all victims. Now, if you'll excuse me, I have places I need to be."

Blunt pushed his way past the officers, who didn't move. When he reached the hallway, Allison Carter was waiting for him. He muttered a few expletives and rolled his eyes.

"I know you have better things to do than harass me, but for some reason, you can't stop," he said.

"No," she said, holding the microphone behind her back. "You're going to tell me how Senator Hirschbeck really died, or I'm going to pin your ass to the wall."

Blunt narrowed his eyes and leaned in close, speaking in a soft voice. "You want to know what happened to Hirschbeck?"

She nodded and whipped her microphone from around her back and placed it near his lips.

"I. Don't. Know."

"Sources tell me that he confronted you about several line items in the defense bill when you were serving together in the senate. Can you confirm or deny that?"

Blunt sighed and eyed her closely. "I gave you the story of the year with Wilson Wellington, yet you haven't pursued it. What did he tell you? What promises did he make you?"

She smiled at him. "I'm going to take that as confirmation that Hirschbeck confronted you."

"Take my response however you wish, but don't dare twist my words. You're going to regret this; that much I can promise you."

He turned in the other direction and kept walking, ignoring her pleas to stop.

What happened to Black?

CHAPTER 29

TITUS BLACK EXITED THE Capitol Building and surveyed the grounds in front of him, searching for anyone who looked remotely like Antoine. The assassin had the capability to incapacitate an entire room at once. While the technology was frightening, Black found it impressive. And though Antoine refused to say whether Dr. Matthews was working with him, a response was no longer necessary. Black was convinced that such a revolutionary and groundbreaking piece of equipment could only be developed by someone with Dr. Matthews's acumen.

What bugged Black the most was trying to figure out where Antoine got the device in the first place. Before he boarded the plane for the U.S., Antoine was thoroughly searched. Then Black was struck by his former captive's deft move.

Diabetes? What a farce—and a genius move, too.

Antoine had preyed on Black's good will and taken

advantage of it. Unable to actually test to see if Antoine had diabetes, the fainting spells and relentless beeping from the supposed blood sugar monitor attached around Antoine's belt provided some measure of necessity. Black never once considered that Antoine could be pretending to have his blood sugar level plummet, coinciding with a slump to the ground. But when Black thought about the situation, he concluded the move was a stroke of genius, almost making him mad that he hadn't thought of a scenario like that first.

Black prided himself on being intuitive to the potential problems swirling around him, especially those related to a captive. But Antoine had managed to pull off the modern-day equivalent of the Trojan Horse. Banned from entering the country, not only had Antoine gained access, he did so all while carting in a device that could render hundreds of people immobile at once. If Antoine wanted to wreak havoc, all he had to do was take his device somewhere with lots of people in a fast-moving situation—Times Square, an airport, a city bus, a subway—and knock them out. And while Black wouldn't put it past Antoine, the evidence seemed to point toward him utilizing it to primarily go after Blunt. Despite the ensuing shootout in the Capitol Building, no one was physically harmed. Stealing an officer's gun and firing it were the two most likely offenses that Antoine committed, nothing that would make him a monster in the eyes of the law. When it came to how society would perceive Antoine's actions versus the allegations hurled at Blunt, the former would manage sympathy while the latter would have the book thrown at him.

Black wasn't going to let that happen. He'd already made the mistake of capturing Antoine and bringing him into the country. But Black needed to atone for such an egregious error. He owed it to Blunt and every other American. A madman like Antoine simply couldn't be allowed to roam free, especially while handling a device that could be used to manipulate hundreds of people and potentially cause them harm.

Black asked Shields what she'd found.

"I've got a big fat nothing burger," she said, "with a side of discouragement and despondency."

"How did he vanish like that?" Black asked.

"Maybe his machine can make him invisible too. There's some technology the military uses now that's very close to making you disappear in plain sight."

"Do you have access to all the CCTV footage in the area?"

"I'm reviewing it as we speak, but I haven't seen anything that looks like him."

Black looked skyward and drew in a deep breath before exhaling. "Maybe he switched outfits or something. I don't know. Just go over it as closely as you can."

"Why don't you get the FBI involved? The more the merrier in a case like this. Plus, the bureau has access to tools that I can't get here."

"If we drag them into it, Antoine is just going to get a bigger audience and more name recognition. We need to take care of this ourselves."

"Have you spoken with Blunt about this yet?"

Black paced around the steps. "He wasn't coherent when I left the room where the hearing was being held. We can talk with him later. Right now, we need to focus our efforts on finding that punk and seeing what we can do about capturing him again."

"I know you're diligently searching for Antoine and want to know his whereabouts, but I have a very serious question that needs to be answered: How come his device had no effect on you?"

"I guess we need to know the origin of its power. In other words, how can that machine make so many people collapse?"

"I've been thinking about this for a while," she said. "And I have a theory."

"Don't hold out on me."

"I read about how ultrasonic warfare is the wave of the future. And everyone within earshot would be subjected to bursts of waves that render them unconscious for a short period of time. Some countries are already using this, though the results have been mixed and testing limited."

"That doesn't explain why I wouldn't have collapsed like everyone else."

"In a way, it does," she said. "How are we communicating right now?"

Black gasped as he realized Shields's discovery. "The coms."

"Exactly. You had something in your ears, which would make it difficult for the waves to penetrate your ear canal."

"So, I guess you're saying don't ever take these things out of my ear?"

She laughed. "Not if you intend to encounter Antoine again."

"I'd love to encounter him right now. But that's the real problem, isn't it?"

Shields sighed. "I'm still not seeing anything remotely resembling him on all the footage I'm scanning."

"Well, don't worry about that," Black said. "I think I know how we can get Antoine to come to us."

"And how do you intend to do that?"

"We're going to tempt him with the thing he wants the most."

"Blunt?"

"Exactly," Black said. "We're going to use Blunt as bait."

CHAPTER 30

WITH ANTOINE IN THE WIND, Black headed to Firestorm headquarters to regroup with Shields and Blunt. During the drive to the office, Black couldn't shake the idea that Blunt was involved in something he shouldn't have been. Blue Moon Rising LLC appeared to have power players and major capital, two elements that set off alarms. If Firestorm had been authorized to eliminate global threats, was it possible Blunt was also helping eliminate political enemies through other means? That was a question Black wanted answered. He had grown fond of Blunt and his no-nonsense approach to dealing with enemies of the U.S. government, both abroad and within the country's borders. But Black didn't want to work for anyone who considered themselves immune from the nation's laws.

When Black entered through the conference room door, Blunt and Shields were already seated at the table. She was drinking a cup of coffee, while Blunt was working over an unlit cigar.

"Just another day at the office for you two, I see," Black said as he took a seat next to Shields.

Blunt sighed and shook his head. "What happened this morning, I've never seen anything like it. Christina has been filling me in on her theory about the technology Antoine used to knock out an entire room. It's truly frightening."

"Who has that kind of technology?" Black asked. "Has our military been developing something like that?"

"I wouldn't be surprised if it was, but Antoine didn't steal this from us—at least, not the technology itself," Blunt said.

"No," Shields said, "he stole one of the world's foremost experts on ultrasonic warfare, Dr. Aaron Matthews."

"That makes sense," Black said. "At least that solves the mystery about whether or not Antoine had him."

Blunt inspected his cigar before cramming it back into his mouth. "But it gets us no closer to finding Dr. Matthews. We need him back on our side so this kind of technology doesn't fall into the wrong hands."

"News about this is already spreading like wildfire," Shields said. "It's all over the internet already.

I dove into the dark web to see if there was any chatter about it there, and there's already an auction set up to purchase that new technology, set to close in two days. The winning bid so far is already well over ten million dollars."

"With that said, we need to figure out a plan to stop him," Blunt said.

Black held up his index finger. "Before we do that, there's something else I need to discuss—we need to discuss—with you."

Blunt scowled. "It can't wait? Apprehending Antoine is top priority."

"Before we proceed, I need a few answers," Black said.

"Answers to what?"

"Questions I have about Blue Moon Rising," Black said.

Blunt leaned back in his chair, clasping his hands together and resting them on his stomach. "What do you want to know?"

"Why are you running a company that gives money to known arms dealers like Orlovsky?" Black asked.

"I can't really talk about what Blue Moon Rising does. All I can say is that sometimes in our line of work, you do things that look suspicious to others but is actually part of a long game. For example, you have met with terrorists in the past, posing as someone else. However, if someone came along and took a picture of you while you were meeting with this terrorist and began to circulate it, some people might get the wrong idea about whose side you're on. Maybe you buy a new house right after this and almost immediately a narrative emerges that you're bought and paid for by a bunch of enemies of the state."

"I get that," Black said. "But there's a big difference between being photographed with someone and actually exchanging hundreds of thousands, if not millions, of dollars. Even you must be able to understand that."

"Draw whatever conclusions you like, but you've known me long enough to know what I'm about. Do I seem like the kind of man who would be fighting terrorists with one hand and then funding them with the other?"

Black shook his head and shifted in his seat. "I never would've considered it before, but Antoine said—"

"Antoine was paid for his work," Blunt said. "And just like every other operative I've brought on, he engaged with me through a trial period. But he was a bit off, too vigilante and money hungry for my tastes. I prefer my agents to be focused on their assignments, not on counting their dollars. And so at the end of the trial period, I told him I didn't have any more new contracts for him, and if I did, I'd give him a call. Since then, I haven't had any use for his services. So, take everything—and I mean everything—he says with a grain of salt. If he can't have things his way, he's going to raze you as he leaves. He's the kind of guy who would take his ball and go home when he was a kid if he didn't like something. Apparently, he didn't like getting left out of Firestorm."

"Does he know about Firestorm?" Shields asked.

Blunt continued chewing on his cigar. "Not by name. He just learned that I ran an under-the-radar agency outside of the normal control channels. I only spoke with him in person once. And there's a firm understanding that if he were to ever divulge this information publicly that there would be grave consequences for his actions."

"Apparently he doesn't care about that anymore," Black said.

"Which is exactly why we need to capture him and eliminate him before he does irreparable damage to the intelligence community," Blunt said. "Based on how things fell into place over the past few days, I can't help but feel like Antoine has been orchestrating this entire moment."

"Even the capture in Merano?" Shields asked.

"Especially that one," Blunt said. "I know he's

been trying to get at me for a while and didn't have a way of getting into the country. So, when I turned down his offer to meet with him in person after the incident in Russia, I'd be willing to bet the farm that Merano wasn't an accidental capture but an intentional set up."

"How could I have missed this?" Black asked.

"It wasn't just you," Blunt said. "It was all of us. To go to such lengths to get captured and dragged across an ocean where there was little chance to escape doesn't seem like a sane plan to us. But then again, we couldn't conceive of a way to knock out everyone in an entire room with the click of a button—and not even pick up a conventional weapon."

"Before we move on, I want to circle back to this Blue Moon Rising situation," Black said. "I want you to look me in the eye and tell me it's a tool you're using to fight terrorism."

"Is this what you need to keep going?" Blunt asked.

Black nodded. "For my sanity."

"Fine," Blunt said. "This is a tool we're using to not just fight but eliminate terrorist cells all over the world. I'll fill you in on all the details when we're done, but in the meantime, just know that everything is legitimate. But the methods we're employing are top secret, even from Congress."

Black eyed Blunt carefully. "Okay, I'm sticking with you on this one. But I'm holding you to your word. I want to learn all about this after we're done. I need to trust that I'm working for someone who truly has this country's best interest at heart."

"I understand," Blunt said. "Now, to the task at hand. Any thoughts on the best way to proceed with our capture of Antoine?"

"Isn't the FBI going to get involved on this one?" Shields asked. "Are our services really necessary?"

"If they catch him, it'll just give him the platform he wants to spew lies about our intelligence community and expose highly guarded secrets," Blunt said. "We need to snag him before anybody else even knows we have him."

"And I know just how to do it," Black said.

"I'm all ears," Blunt said.

"You may not like this," Shields said. "So, brace yourself."

Blunt chuckled. "How bad could it be?"

"We want to use you as bait," Black said.

"You think he wants me that bad?" Blunt said, pointing to his chest "I thought he wanted to publicly embarrass and ridicule me."

"Which he already did," Black said. "But he also wants you dead, which you would be if I'd succumbed to his ultrasonic weapon. Fortunately, that wasn't the case. But he's going after you full bore."

"And you think we're just going to lure him in like a fly to honey?" Blunt asked.

Black nodded. "Did you ever meet him anywhere?"

"My mountain home near Fort Valley. It's technically a safe house I've utilized to host contract workers. We met there once."

"Think he would look for you there?" Shields asked.

"If we got a message to him that I'd be there," Blunt said.

Black chuckled. "You have his cell phone number?"

"I don't need it," Blunt said. I just need to tell the right person where I'm gonna be."

Shields scribbled down some notes. "Look, you do realize that if you do this, it's likely going to mean that this place is burned for you?"

"I'm fine with that," he said. "We need to catch this bastard before he does anything else."

"Who's the right person to tell that you're going to be there?" Black asked.

Blunt stroked his chin as his gaze met Black's. "I've been thinking about this. If Antoine planned all this, someone with intimate knowledge of the hearing had to be letting him know all the details like where to be and what time to be there. Everything was hush-hush up until a few days ago. So, if he was planning to ambush me publicly, how would he have been able to do it unless someone told him when and where I'd be, someone who helped set all of this up."

Black set his jaw and shook his head subtly. "Wilson Wellington."

Blunt nodded in agreement. "That bastard has been orchestrating this from the very beginning."

"And you think he'll get a message to Antoine for you?" Shields asked.

"Most assuredly after the news about his involvement in a cover-up scheme from the war breaks tomorrow," Blunt said. "He'll likely do whatever he can to strike back and strip me of my power. But it'll be too late for him to do anything meaningful to me."

"I thought Allison Carter wasn't helping you out?" Shields asked.

"She's not, so I shared the information with another reporter," Blunt said. "There's going to be a big exposé published any moment now—at least, that's what I've been told. And if it is, then we can bank on Wellington finding a way to get that piece of information to Antoine."

Black nodded. "In that case, looks like you've got a call to make—and some bags to pack."

CHAPTER 31

MICHELLE MORGAN SPENT HER entire morning on the phone, chasing down leads and trying to get people to comment on the story that fell into her lap before she even bought a cup of coffee. Her phone had rung just as she was getting out of bed with a call from a number she didn't recognize. Five minutes later, a former senator she'd once profiled, J.D. Blunt, was giving her the scoop of a lifetime. And as a recent hire for the Associated Press's Washington bureau, the story was something she desperately needed to establish herself as a hard-hitting reporter.

During his time in congress, Wilson Wellington had developed such a reputation for his ability to survive scandals that he'd been given the nickname "The Teflon Man" by Morgan's fellow media members. No amount of extramarital affairs with staffers or campaign finance charges or censures from his fellow senators were enough to get the voters from his state to send him packing. He seemed so immune to damning behavior that most reporters around Washington barely even raised an eyebrow when a new indiscretion became public. But this one felt different. This was the cover-up of a setup, a plot to murder someone.

All Morgan had to do was fill in the blanks, something even Blunt couldn't do.

As she pored over the report Blunt had emailed, she couldn't help but wonder what could motivate a military commander to send one of his own into the line of fire, knowing he wouldn't come back alive. For all intents and purposes, the action constituted setting up a murder, a crime far more nefarious than simply arranging for campaign contributions to get funneled into re-election coffers. A man was dead because of what Wellington did. While his constituents might shrug, a military tribunal wouldn't. His position since moving into civilian life wouldn't matter either.

Morgan called several of the men mentioned in the sealed report. Her investigative skills proved Blunt gave the information to the right reporter as she managed to wrangle three of the four officers mentioned in the official documents. She found the fact that a judge had sealed the personnel record of Captain Black from reaching the light of day equally troubling. At least the truth had a chance to come out now.

The detail that made the story extra scandalous was the one omitted from everything Morgan had received from Blunt. And it was the one element that everyone would want to know—the why. Why would a commander sabotage one of his most decorated pilots? Why would a leader entrenched in a war make such a selfish decision? And why would Wellington try to hide it?

Morgan found one officer, Jarrett Gordon, willing to tell it all on the condition of anonymity. Apparently, there were several people who knew, but he told her that if they talked longer than a minute on his cell phone, "people would find out."

Gordon was working at the Pentagon but called in sick so he could meet Morgan for an early morning meeting over coffee. What he told her left her shocked and disheartened.

"I hope you nail that bastard to the wall," Gordon said. "He was always condescending and arrogant toward nearly everyone. Everyone in the squadron had grown tired of him as the war came to an end."

"I'm not interested in settling a personal vendetta," Morgan said. "I just want the truth."

"You already have it. I just hope you do something with it. I've told this story to three other reporters. Two of them ended up dead. The other one lives in a waterfront house in Hawaii. Draw your own conclusions from that."

Morgan swallowed hard. "How did anyone know you spoke with them?"

"I'm guessing someone with access to my phone records. That's why I wanted to talk in person. The other three times, I conducted the interviews on the phone. If you called the other officers mentioned in the report, nobody will suspect a thing."

"Except that you did speak with me briefly."

Gordon shrugged. "Wellington cobbled together a life founded on lies and murder. What kind of journalist would you be if you just walked away from this story? The only way to protect yourself is to run it as soon as possible. The other reporters all sat on this information, hoping to get more confirmation. What they got was either a bullet to the head or a hefty gift that landed them on a tropical island in the Pacific. I'm sure you'd rather have a Pulitzer."

"I'll settle for the truth," she said.

"Well, you got it from me. Now what you do with it is up to you."

Morgan nodded and wasted no time returning to her office to pound out a story that she knew was going to lead every broadcast and garner headlines in every paper across the country. Once people learned that Wellington was a murderer, the country would go mad—even if he was the odds on favorite to oust Michaels from the White House. Somebody needed to do something. She figured it might as well be her.

As Morgan pecked away on her keyboard, her fingers trembled. The words on the screen seemed surreal, an article that seemed perfectly at home in a country eroding with corruption. But not the United States. She struggled to believe what she wrote, even though she was merely relaying the facts that had been given to her.

Senator Wellington Battlefield Murder Covered Up blared her headline. The editors would likely choose something different. That was their job. Hers was to piece together the kind of story that would serve the public's best interest. All the clicks and traffic on the website were simply a nice bonus.

"Lead with the who and the what, follow with the why," her favoring journalism teacher preached while she attended the Missouri School of Journalism at the University of Missouri. She exhaled when she sent the story to her editor. But she grinned when the story was posted to the website three hours later, just before everyone's afternoon commute. Her editors had become pros on knowing the right moment to garner the most attention for a bombshell story such as this one. As she read the headline and first paragraph, her heart pounded, not out of anticipation for how the rest of Washington would react to the accusations, but out of fear that Wellington or someone else might actually try to kill her.

Senator Wellington Under Fire for Wartime Murder blared the new headline, which was happily accompanied by a brief header to explain what was really happening.

"Wellington had hand in death of pilot, records show" read the short tagline. She took a deep breath and re-read the first part of her story.

> Senator Wilson Wellington escaped punishment after sending a pilot into a no-fly zone over Afghanistan that resulted in his death more than fifteen years ago, personnel records show that recently came to light.
>
> Sources involved in the incident confirmed what has been hidden in sealed military files for years. A spokesperson with Wellington's office denied that the senator committed any wrongdoing during his stint as an officer in the U.S. Air Force during the conflict.
>
> The pilot, Captain Victor Black, reportedly learned of Wellington's affair with a subordinate and threatened to report it. However, court records show that Wellington's

father, Rutherford Wellington, the former senator who at one time chaired the Armed Services committee, pressured high-ranking officials to suppress the report and lighten the punishment for his son. Rutherford died in a hunting accident a year ago.

Her eyes widened, almost in disbelief that the story was true, much less that she'd written it. But every word of it had been verified by multiple sources—and there was no doubt that not even The Teflon Man could survive such a story.

In a matter of hours, if not minutes, Wilson Wellington was about to be done in Washington.

CHAPTER 32

BLUNT THREW HIS BAG into the trunk and then slammed it shut. While he was anxious to capture and eliminate Antoine, Blunt didn't like being dangled as bait. He trusted Black or else he never would've agreed to the plan, but Blunt couldn't shake the uneasy feeling he had. If one thing went wrong, the consequences could cost him his life. He'd already been granted one reprieve during the committee hearing, and he wasn't thrilled about the idea of charging back into harm's way. Yet given how quickly they needed to contain the situation—both for his sake and the sake of the country—he didn't feel like he had much of a choice.

"Are you ready for this?" Shields asked as Blunt opened his car door.

"Is anyone ever prepared to be used to draw out a trained assassin?" he asked, patting his chest now protected by a bulletproof vest.

"You don't have to wear that now," she said. "I

know how hot those things are. You can just put it on when we get to the house."

"I know it's silly, but it makes me feel a little safer. I know those guys are trained to shoot targets in the head. However, if he misses, I'd love to have a fighting chance."

Shields took his hands, her gaze meeting his. "Nothing's going to happen to you. We got this. You're working with two professionals who are going to do everything in our power to make sure you get out of there without a scratch. Do you understand?"

Blunt nodded. "It's still a risk."

"You know we'd do anything else if there was another way to bring this situation to a quick resolution, right?"

"Of course. Let's just go nail Antoine and get this thing over with."

Shields released his hands and spun toward her SUV, where Black was waiting. Blunt watched her walk away, basking in the moment of gratitude to have people around him who weren't just operatives. They were his family, and they'd do anything for each other.

Blunt jerked the door open and climbed behind the steering wheel. He glanced at his phone, which had several text messages from lawmakers he'd worked with who were in shock about the breaking news regarding Wilson Wellington. As Blunt turned out of his driveway, he picked up his phone and prepared to dial Wellington's number. But Blunt didn't have to. His cell vibrated in his hand with an incoming call.

"This is Blunt," he said, answering and then placing the call on speaker phone.

Wellington opened with a string of expletives, calling Blunt just about every derogatory name he'd ever heard.

Sounds like some of my former constituents.

When Wellington took a breath, Blunt responded. "Are you done?"

"No, I'm not, but I don't have the time to sufficiently describe what kind of person you are."

Blunt cracked a faint smile. "I warned you, but you didn't listen. You only have yourself to blame."

"I couldn't stop Elliott. He decided to press on despite my best efforts to persuade him to do something else."

"I wish I could believe you, Wilson. But after what happened today, I'd be a fool to."

"What are you talking about?"

"That ambush at the hearing was a disgusting personal attack," Blunt said as he navigated his car onto the freeway. "And there's only one person who could've fed that information to Elliott."

"Where are you right now? We need to discuss this in person."

"I've got to get out of town for a few days, get out in nature, clear my head," Blunt said. "Maybe when I get back."

"This can't wait."

"It's going to have to," Blunt said. "I don't want reporters camping out around my house."

"Neither do I. But that's going to be the case, thanks to you. They'll all be there to capture the moment the authorities come to arrest me for this sham. You don't know the whole story. That report didn't have everything in it."

"You think that's going to make me call some media outlets and recant these accusations?" Blunt asked with a chuckle. "Forget about it. Now, after you've cool down for a few days, maybe we can have an adult conversation about this issue. But nothing is going to change the fact of what you did, no matter what the reason was—or what else I don't know."

Blunt hung up and smiled. The trap had been laid; the message had been sent.

And in Blunt's mind, there was no doubt Wellington was already dialing Antoine's number.

CHAPTER 33

Sperryville, Virginia

ANTOINE PARKED HIS VEHICLE well off the main road and covered the sides of his SUV with branches and limbs. It wasn't the best camouflage job he'd ever done, but Antoine didn't intend on staying much past dark. He planned to make his conversation with Blunt a short one. Plenty of begging and pleading, maybe even some genuine tears from the former Texas senator before Antoine pulled the trigger. He already had the moment planned out. The shot was going to be perfectly placed, guaranteeing maximum pain from a slow bleed. Antoine wasn't usually so cruel, but his life had been ruined by Blunt. So he deserved every bit of it, even the humiliating finale.

As Antoine crept through the woods toward the target location, he recalled the entire exchange that day between him and Blunt.

When Blunt first made eye contact at their meeting at a coffee shop in College Park, he wore a scowl on his face. Antoine had just watched someone serve Blunt with papers in the parking. He also had salsa stains on his white shirt, which he later explained happened while trying to avoid a jaywalker in early morning traffic.

"Maybe we need to trade places for a few hours," Antoine suggested.

Blunt looked around before leaning across the table and hunching low. "You think killing someone is going to help me have a better day?"

"Depends on who you're killing," Antoine said.

"That's a fact," Blunt said. "I know one guy in particular whose death might turn this entire day around."

"Who's that?"

"Senator Guy Hirschbeck."

Antoine chuckled. "Any man named 'Guy' probably deserves to die an excruciating and painful death."

"Someone with that name beat you while you were growing up?" Blunt asked.

Antoine's face went white. "No, at least not on a regular basis. Why would you ask that?"

"That's some strong pent-up animosity toward someone simply because of their name."

Antoine rolled up his sleeve and traced a long scar that ran from his elbow to his wrist. "That's from a man named Guy. Another slash of his knife nearly caught me in the neck, but I jumped back just in time to avoid it."

"Was this on a mission of yours?"

Antoine shook his head. "At a pub one night after this guy started in on me about a comment I made to the bartender."

"How'd it end?"

"Three people pulled me off him or else I would've killed him that night."

Blunt stroked his chin. "So, is this profession of yours now a type of therapy?"

Antoine lied. "Absolutely not. I don't show emotion any more. What I do now is strictly business."

He wasn't about to concede that he still felt rage along with a sense of satisfaction every time he watched his targets gasp for their last breath.

"Well, if you killed a man named Guy, I certainly wouldn't complain," Blunt said with a chuckle.

That was the only comment Blunt made, moving along to the target Antoine was actually hired to take out. But Antoine sensed that was more than a passing mention. Two days later, he staged a carjacking to make every agency believe that Senator Hirschbeck had been nothing more than the victim of a random robbery. Blunt never said anything to Antoine about it, but he felt like Blunt knew.

But over the following weeks, Antoine became more and more intimately acquainted with Blunt's methods, including the ways he distributed funds for completed jobs. Through research and attentive observation, Antoine realized that Blunt acted as if he was autonomous, answering to no one. And the day Antoine dared to question Blunt, their entire professional relationship changed. No more openness. No more discussing personal life. No more acting normal and carrying on. Two days after that, Antoine was accused of an attempted assassination. While the U.S. government considered extradition, someone with enough clout persuaded the FBI to leave him banned from the country and decided to work with Interpol to capture him in Europe. The problem with their plan was that Antoine was too slippery.

And now it was time to make Blunt pay for everything.

After stealthily navigating the Blue Ridge Mountains, Antoine settled into the natural blind he found in the wood about two hundred yards away from Blunt's mountain cabin. The two men had met at the place once before, but this time Antoine wasn't coming at the behest of Blunt. Antoine pulled out his binoculars to inspect the target. The former Texas senator was sitting on the porch, reading a John Grisham novel and sipping on a glass of bourbon.

You have no idea what's coming.

A stiff breeze rushed fallen leaves along the ground in the twilight. Antoine wondered if anyone else was here. But he'd done his due diligence before even venturing out. Blunt's house was secluded, and for good reason. The nearest neighbor was more than a mile on either side of him.

Antoine opened his rifle case and assembled his weapon. Peering through his scope, he sighted in Blunt. All Antoine had to do was slide a bullet into the chamber and pull the trigger. Everything would be over in an instant. But that's not how he was going to say his goodbyes to Blunt. Not after the way he'd treated Antoine, turning him into a fugitive. Not after the way Blunt acted as if he were God, exacting payback against his political rivals. No, the way that Blunt chose to eliminate Antoine was cruel, allowing him to live while making him a fugitive.

Before Antoine finished the job, they needed to talk first. Or more precisely, Blunt needed to beg and plead after he asked for forgiveness.

Antoine slung his rifle over his shoulder and headed toward the house. He stepped lightly as he went, careful not to snap any twigs and alert Blunt that an intruder had invaded the premises.

By bringing Antoine back to U.S. soil, Blunt had unwittingly set up his own demise.

And Antoine couldn't wait to finish off the man who'd destroyed his life.

CHAPTER 34

BLACK PEERED THROUGH the slats in Blunt's garden shed situated about fifty yards away from the back of the house. A porch wrapped all the way around the house, and Blunt sat at the rear reading a book. The land immediately surrounding the mountain home was cleared but dotted with small clumps of pine trees and occasional oaks and other hardwoods, while the perimeter was a thick forest. From Black's position, he had a clear view of Blunt and would be able to see anyone approaching. However, the sun had just dipped beneath the tallest peak, and daylight was quickly giving way to dusk.

"Are you sure this plan is going to work?" Blunt asked over the coms, covering his mouth as he spoke.

"We set traps and hope they work," Black said. "According to Mallory Kauffman who was monitoring Wellington's communications for us, we know that he texted someone giving them the time and location of the hearing that morning. We also know that Antoine is a known associate of Wellington's. According to one report I read, Wellington hired Antoine to, quote unquote, handle some issues."

"And you're sure Wellington would tell Antoine about this?"

"I'm betting my career and your life on it," Black said.

"Not exactly a fair gamble."

"We've got your back," Shields chimed in. "Just whatever you do, keep that ear piece inserted."

"Roger that," Blunt said. "I'm going inside to fix some tea and keep reading. It's getting a little bit too chilly even with this jacket on."

Black had set up a perimeter alarm earlier in the day and tested it several times to make sure everything functioned properly. All he could do was sit and wait. And while he took no joy in eliminating Antoine, killing him was a necessity. Plenty of doubt had already been cast on Blunt, which didn't sit well with Black. He accepted Blunt's explanation for now, but working with integrity, even while scribbling outside the lines of the law, was important. Getting the job done and keeping people safe was the mission, not settling personal scores. If that's what Blunt was doing, Black knew he would have a problem with it. But those were answers he'd never get if he didn't protect his boss first. Antoine had gone from helpful ally to loose cannon. And there was only one way to stop him.

Five minutes went by with nothing but the sound of crispy leaves trickling across the ground and a few squirrels chattering in a nearby treetop.

"Is he ever going to get here?" Shields asked.

"Just be patient," Black said. "He'll be here before you know it."

A few more minutes passed before Black's phone buzzed with an alert. The perimeter had been broken.

"He's here," Black whispered.

"Roger that," Shields said.

"Blunt? You there?" he asked.

"I heard you," Blunt said.

"Get to the room we talked about," Black said.

"Heading there now."

Darkness had now fallen, making it increasingly difficult to see. Black pulled his infrared glasses down from his forehead and secured them around his eyes. He didn't see any heat signatures in his line of sight.

"Are you watching on satellite?" Black asked Shields, who was in a surveillance van about a hundred yards off the road, hidden among the trees.

"Yeah, but I don't see anything."

"Nothing?"

"Not that would indicate there's another person out there."

"Maybe it was an animal or something," Black said. "I'll reset it."

He typed in a few commands from his phone.

That ought to do it.

"Wait a minute," Shields said. "I've got some movement on the west side of the house. Definitely not an animal."

Black eased out of the shed and hustled in the direction Shields mentioned.

"Blunt, are you in the saferoom," he whispered.

"Already there," Blunt said.

Black scanned the area, still not seeing anyone. "How did he slip by us?"

"There are ways to mask your heat," Shields said. "And this guy is a former elite Russian operative. Did you think this was going to be easy?"

"I was hoping," Black said. "Where'd he go?"

"He's going inside," she said.

Black cursed under his breath as he broke into a sprint. The protocol they'd set up was designed to keep Blunt out of harm's way in the event of a perimeter breach. But Black never believed that was likely to happen. Between Shields's overhead satellite images and his monitoring the area in infrared, what was the chance that Antoine could get so close to the house without anyone noticing first? Yet somehow he had.

"Get out of there now," Black said over the coms.

"What about the panic room?" Blunt asked.

"It's not going to matter if he gets to you first," Black said. "And I can't even see him yet."

"I knew this was a terrible idea," Blunt said.

"Just get your weapon and get to the woods."

As Black reached the west side of the house, he heard Blunt's voice over the coms again.

"I'm clear," Blunt said.

"Roger that," Black said. "I'm going after Antoine."

"The target just went inside," Shields said.

Black saw Blunt dart out of the back door and hustle toward the woods.

"Stay out of sight until I give you the signal that the coast is clear," Black said.

Black entered the house through the front door, which Antoine had left open. A creaking noise emanated from the stairs, giving away Antoine's position. Black glided across the floor, his gun trained forward. However, as he rounded the corner and peered up the steps, they were empty.

Where'd he go?

A thump from the living room drew Black's attention as he switched directions and followed the sounds from the old house that had been built nearly a century ago. He reached the doorway leading inside the den but stopped short, instead poking his head around the corner to see if Antoine was there. He spun around at the same moment as Black, and the two men locked eyes. Antoine was covered in body armor and even wore a helmet.

"Not who you were looking for?" Black asked.

They both had their weapons aimed at each other, neither giving any indication of what they were about to do next.

"Your little magic tricks aren't going to work on me this time either," Black said.

Antoine ignored Black's barb. "Where is he?"

"Where's who?"

"Don't play dumb with me. You know who I'm talking about."

Black shrugged. "If you're referring to Blunt, he's not here."

"You're gonna take me to him."

"I don't think so," Black said. "This ends right here, right now."

"Not for me it doesn't," Antoine said.

He didn't wait for a response before opening fire. Black darted around the side of the wall, poking his head around to catch a glimpse of Antoine and shoot back. For the next couple minutes, the two men exchanged rounds. Then Black ducked back behind the wall, ripped a flashbang out of a grenade holster, pulled the pin, and flung the weapon toward Antoine.

Black didn't wait before charging straight toward the attacker, who was disoriented from the explosion. When Black hit Antoine, he staggered backward, slamming his head into the wall. But Antoine absorbed the hit and spun to the side. Black had latched onto Antoine's bulletproof vest and rode him down to the ground, forcing him onto his back.

With Black on top and in control, he reached for his gun to end the confrontation, but Antoine seized the opportunity to punch Black in the throat. Stunned from the blow, he grabbed at his neck and coughed reflexively. The natural reaction made Black vulnerable, which Antoine took advantage of by reaching for Black's left ear and prying loose one of the coms. Then Antoine reached for his pocket.

Black was briefly baffled by the move before he realized what was happening. He plugged his left ear with his middle finger and then tried to prevent Antoine from setting off his devastating device. Once he pulled it out of his pocket, Black jammed his knee into Antoine's forearm, forcing him to release his grip on the device. Black swatted it aside before putting his hands around Antoine's neck.

However, Antoine kept fighting, pushing Black's jaw until his chin moved up into a painful and awkward position.

Black rolled off Antoine in an attempt to regain control. But Antoine dove for the mechanism and tried to push it. Black plugged his ear just in time and then pulled out his gun. Antoine threw his hands in the air in a posture of surrender.

"Blunt isn't who you think he is," Antoine said. "You're going to find that out soon enough—and you're going to regret it."

"I doubt it," Black said.

Then he pulled the trigger, hitting Antoine in the head.

Black waited a moment as blood pooled around his target. After half a minute, Black checked Antoine's pulse. He was gone.

"The target is down," Black said.

"And you?" Shields asked.

"I'll live," Black said. "Did you hear that, Blunt?"

There wasn't a reply.

"Blunt?" Shields asked.

A gunshot from outside pierced the evening sky.

CHAPTER 35

"WHAT WAS THAT?" Black asked into his coms.

"There's another hostile on the property with Blunt," Shields said. "I didn't see him until just now. I was watching your body cam."

Black cursed as he sprinted toward the rendezvous point he'd sent Blunt.

"I'm sorry," Shields said. "I didn't consider anyone else would've come with him."

"Where are they?" Black asked.

"Behind the shed."

The possibility that Antoine would bring help didn't occur to Black either, if he was being honest. Once he had Antoine cornered and Blunt out of the house, there shouldn't have been any reason to worry. But now Black was facing the possibility that using Blunt as bait would cost him his life.

Black raced toward the utility structure he'd used just a half-hour ago to watch Blunt's house. When

Black arrived, he found Blunt with his hands in the air, back against the building. In front of him was none other than Wilson Wellington, his pistol trained on Blunt.

"Put the gun down," Wellington said, cutting his eyes toward Black. "At least if you don't want your boss here to die."

Black lowered his weapon. "It's over, Senator," he said. "Antoine is dead."

"It's not over for me, thanks to this man right here," Wellington said. "In fact, it's only just beginning because of that bombshell report about my actions during the war in Afghanistan."

Black narrowed his eyes. "You killed my father."

"The Taliban killed your father, not me."

"You sent him there, knowing he would die."

Wellington shook his head. "You don't understand. I didn't have a choice."

Black shook his head. "We always have a choice. You made the wrong one. And the sooner you can accept that, the better off you'll be. Trying to blame others for your own transgressions isn't going to change the fact that you sent a man into battle knowing he was going to die."

"Your boss here is responsible for all of this mess," Wellington said. "Isn't that right, J.D.? Tell him."

Blunt shook his head. "He's delusional. Don't believe a word out of his mouth."

"No, I'm not," Wellington said. "J.D., you're the one who has a bad habit of instigating needless tragedy in people's lives."

"Is this true?" Black asked.

"Absolutely not," Blunt said.

"Liar," Wellington roared. "That was all tied to Blue Moon Rising. Did you investigate that, Mr. Black?"

Black eyed Blunt, who shook his head subtly. "Blue Moon Rising was active during the war?"

Wellington nodded. "They've been creating chaos in various forms for nearly half a century, all under the cover of the intelligence community."

"I don't know who told you this, but that's simply not true."

"It is," Wellington said. "And I'll prove it to you. Both of you, to the house. And put the weapon away, Mr. Black."

Black holstered his gun and raised his hands, following Blunt to the house. Once they got inside, Wellington directed his two hostages to sit on the couch in the living room.

"Now, you two have a simple choice," Wellington said. "Call the reporter who you gave all that bogus information to and tell her it was all a fabrication. Or

I will destroy both your lives."

Blunt shook his head. "I can't do that."

"Maybe you didn't hear me when I gave you your two choices," Wellington said.

"I did, but I'm opting for a third choice," Blunt said.

"And what choice is that?" Wellington asked.

Blunt smiled wryly. "Not lift a finger to refute anything you've said and walk out of here."

"That's not a wise decision," Wellington said. "Upon my death, records will be released showing exactly what I'm saying tonight and proving what a hypocrite you are."

Blunt crossed his arms and shook his head. "You're peddling lies, Wilson. You can't own up to your mistakes. Everyone will see right through this desperate attempt of yours to shift the blame and cast yourself as a victim. Nobody is going to believe you, even if you were telling the truth."

"But I am, and you know it. I guess you don't care what your little minions will think when the reality about who you are is laid bare before the world. And this guy here certainly won't find out who's really responsible for his father's death or the secret he found out that cost him his life."

Black thought he saw a shadow just outside the window and shot a glance toward it. He noticed a silhouette with a gun and realized it was Shields. He lifted a hand up, trying to play off the gesture as just fidgeting. But Shields would get the message, realizing he was waving her off. When Wellington looked at Blunt, Black took a quick peek at the window and noticed Shields had lowered her pistol.

"Stop playing games," Blunt said. "Your pathetic attempt to distort reality isn't going to work on Agent Black. He's too smart to fall for your attempts to twist the truth."

"No, no," Black said. "I want to hear what the senator has to say about this. If there's more to the story, I want to hear it."

Wellington wagged his finger. "Not until Blunt calls that reporter and tells her that he was lying."

Blunt shook his head. "What I told her was a hundred percent factual."

"When the truth comes out, they're going to hunt you down just like they're coming after me."

"Tell me more about my father," Black asked. "I need to know."

"That's up to J.D., and apparently he doesn't want to play along," Wellington said. "So, there's only one thing to do."

Wellington steadied his gun on Blunt. "I'm going to get revenge."

"You don't have to do this," Black said. "You

have a gun trained on you right now. So, I suggest you lower your weapon."

Wellington pressed the barrel of his pistol against his head. "Why? Because someone might shoot me? I'm going out on my terms. And you're gonna have one helluva time explaining how I ended up dead in your house, J.D."

"No, don't—"

Wellington didn't hesitate, pulling the trigger and then crumpling to the floor.

Black rushed over to Wellington. And it was like his lifeless eyes wanted to say something else, but they didn't have the chance.

Black looked up at Blunt and glared at him. "What did you do?"

"That was a fine theatrical performance," Blunt said. "Nothing more, nothing less. There's nothing for him to tell."

"He seemed to think there was more to my father's death than what was in that report," Black said. "And he more than implied that you had something to do with it."

"If there's more to it, I don't know anything about it. But I can promise you that I wasn't involved in any way. I didn't even know your father. You have to believe me."

Black stood up and sighed. Shields rushed inside,

her weapon still drawn.

"Is everyone okay?" she asked, giving Black a long hug. "I thought I was too late."

Blunt nodded. "We're good. But we've got a mess we need to clean up. I need to make some calls to get this taken care of."

He sauntered outside, dialing a number on his cell as he went.

"What about you?" she asked, removing her coms. "I heard everything Wellington was saying."

"I don't know what to think," Black said, ripping his coms out of his ear. "But I'm pretty convinced there's probably more to it than what was in my father's sealed personnel records."

"And what about Blue Moon Rising?" she asked.

"We need to keep digging," Black said.

He shuffled into the kitchen and found the device that he'd been fighting over with Antoine just a few minutes earlier. After picking it up, he inspected the name embossed on it: Colton Industries.

"Would you look at this?" Black said.

Shields hustled to him and stared at the words just above Black's index finger before reading them aloud. "Colton Industries," she said. "Mean anything to you?"

"Other than the fact that they are one of the leading weapons manufacturers in the world, I guess not much."

"So, you're thinking maybe Dr. Matthews didn't help Antoine make this device?"

Black looked closer and shook his head. "Upon further inspection, not anymore."

"What do you mean?" she asked as she withdrew.

"Look at these initials burned into the bottom of the casing here," he said. "D—A—M. That's all the proof we need to know that he was likely involved: Dr. Aaron Matthews."

CHAPTER 36

BLUNT LUMBERED TO THE EDGE of his property and watched the moon rise on the horizon. Below the twinkling lights of the Shenandoah Valley yielded to the illusion that his land was secluded. The forests and trees provided sufficient cover from the city just over two hours away that loved to feast on a person's soul before discarding them. If there was one thing Blunt had learned after all his years in the nation's capital, it's that everyone comes to Washington thinking they're going to change the world. They either leave disillusioned and disenfranchised—or corrupted to the core. No matter how much Wellington and Antoine tried to cast aspersions on others, the two dead men were responsible for their own decisions. Ultimately, their quest for power and position and fortune had lured them with great promise only to deliver an early demise.

And Blunt didn't want to catch any of the blowback for their deaths as they made a desperate attempt to bring him down in their final acts.

He fished around in his pocket for a cigar before pulling one out and popping it into his mouth. Next, he dialed Besserman's number and waited for him to answer.

"Where are you?" Besserman asked. "I've been trying to get a hold of you for hours."

"I've been a little busy. What's going on?"

"The FBI has launched a manhunt for Wilson Wellington since he didn't turn himself at the time his lawyer had worked out," Besserman said. "I know you were trying to take care of Antoine, but Wellington might be coming for you now too. But more than anything, I'm glad to find out that you're safe."

"I wish I'd answered my phone then," Blunt said. "We already found him."

"You have Wellington?"

"In a manner of speaking, which is actually why I was calling you. He's dead."

"What? How?"

"Self-inflicted gunshot to the head, done right there in the middle of my living room," Blunt said. "And now I'm gonna need help from one of your cleanup teams."

"That bad, huh?"

"I don't want any law enforcement officers snooping around here. Two people dead on my property in the same day—and outspoken critics of mine in recent days—that's not exactly a good look."

"And all it'll take is one bulldog investigator to sink his teeth into these cases and we'll never get free," Besserman said.

"I'm glad you understand and that we're on the same page on this one," Blunt said. "If someone came up here trying to dig up dirt on me, I'm sure they'd find some facts to twist and repackage and then sell them as the truth."

"We'll handle it. Just get the hell outta there before the cleanup crew arrives. We don't want your paths to ever cross."

"Got it. We're leaving now. And, Bobby—"

"Yeah?"

"I've got a question about something Wellington said."

"Fire away."

Blunt balled up his left hand and blew into it, warming it up. "Wellington suggested that Blue Moon Rising existed before we incorporated it. Do you know anything about that?"

"There was another group before us, but it's not the same. He was just trying to rattle your cage before he died. The world will remember him as the murderer and coward that he was."

"And you're sure there's nothing more to that case than what was in Captain Black's personnel records?"

"Not to my knowledge," Besserman said. "There could be more to it, but I've never heard any whispers about some cover up related to this story until recently."

"Wellington scolded us for exposing him, warning us that there was more to the story."

"And what did he tell you?"

"He shot himself after that grand announcement," Blunt said.

"Don't worry about it. He was just trying to get in your head."

Blunt sighed. "I'll try to forget about it. But when I get back to Washington, we need to talk about how we're going to handle this with the press."

"You're right. We need to pass along some more stories about Wellington so everybody knows what kind of man he was."

"Agreed," Blunt said. "I'll contact you when I get there."

Blunt hustled back toward the house. When he entered, he found Black and Shields talking while standing just a few feet over Wellington's dead body.

"We need to move," Blunt said. "A cleanup team

is on its way, and we don't need to be here when they get here."

"Who were you talking to?" Shields asked.

"Besserman," Blunt said.

"Did you ask him about what Wellington said?" Black asked.

"Yeah, and he essentially said that Wellington was full of it, just trying to rattle our cages."

"Now we need to go," Blunt said.

"But what about Dr. Matthews?" Shields asked.

Blunt shrugged. "Who knows? We're no closer to Dr. Matthews's location today than we were when this entire mess started. He could be holed up in a basement in Washington just as easily as he could be tucked away in a research facility in St. Petersburg."

"Maybe not," Shields said, holding up the small box that Antoine had passed off as his blood sugar monitor. "Did you check out this device Antoine was using to incapacitate everyone?"

Blunt took the box and inspected it. "Is there something I should be looking for on this thing?"

"Yeah, right there," Shields said, pointing to the bottom of the mechanism. "It's got the Colton Industries logo embossed on the casing."

Blunt inspected it more closely and then handed it back to Shields. "That's a fake."

"A fake?"

"It's a knockoff. Someone is trying to throw you off," Blunt said. "And it's Dr. Aaron Matthews."

"Well that's just wonderful," Shields said. "That leaves us right back where we started."

Blunt pulled his cigar out of his mouth and grunted. "No, this is a clue. And I know exactly where he is."

CHAPTER 37

Three days later
Sillamäe, Estonia

BLACK CLIMBED A SPRUCE TREE that ascended well above the cinderblock fence designed to keep prying eyes from seeing into the guarded space. The needle-laden branches provided sufficient cover for him as he peered inside the confines and tried to figure out the best approach to gain entry.

What Black found was a loading dock that appeared abandoned, punctuated by rusted handrails and weathered concrete. There wasn't a soul in sight.

"I'm beginning to wonder if Blunt knew what he was talking about with this one," Black said over his coms.

"I don't see any activity from my views on the satellite feeds either," Shields said.

"No guards, no vehicles. It's a virtual ghost town."

"Should I call Blunt and tell him his hunch was

wrong on this one?"

"Let's give it some time," Black said. "I'll continue surveillance and see if we get any movement."

The reason they were Estonia in the first place seemed like a shot in the dark. When Blunt studied the ultrasonic device Antoine had used to incapacitate people, he noticed a piece of loparite, a rare earth element, embedded in the device. Blunt said during the height of the Cold War, the Soviet Union operated one plant in Estonia that handled loparite, using it to help with the process of enriching uranium. Yet after Estonia gained its independence and the plant shuttered, the compound remained a suspected location for nefarious activity by the CIA, including black market uranium enrichment. Combined with the fact that the location wasn't that far from where Antoine had lured them to in the first place, Blunt was convinced that was where Dr. Matthews was being held.

A half-hour passed, and Black hadn't seen any movement.

"According to the intelligence report, there are only three guards inside," Shields said. "But I'm beginning to think there aren't any. Maybe we should just pack it in. Blunt won't like it, but I think he got this one wrong."

"I think you might be—" Black said before stopping. "Hold on. I think I see something."

Black scanned the area below through his binoculars and noticed someone at the front perimeter fence, which led into the empty back parking lot. However, a small gate for pedestrians swung open and he ducked inside.

"I'm watching it too," she said.

The man, who was carrying a briefcase, strode around to the back of the building and entered a number on a keypad beside a door. The door flew outward, and a guard with a machine gun slung over his shoulder glanced around the parking lot as he ushered the man inside.

"Bingo," Black said. "I've got the access number."

"At least we know there's one armed guard," Shields said. "Think this might be the right place now?"

"We're about to find out."

Black shimmied down to the ground and climbed over the fence. He hustled up to the keypad and entered the number. Once inside, he was greeted by a musty smell and a dark corridor with flickering fluorescent lights. He trained his weapon in front of him as he moved forward.

He turned left and found a set of stairs. Upon

descending to the bottom floor, Black turned down the hallway and found a lab. He peeked through the glass window and found a half-dozen people clad in white coats, analyzing objects underneath microscopes, operating centrifuges, and recording results on clipboards. At the far end of the room, two armed men hovered over the workers.

Black was still surveying the activity inside when a man rounded the corner and shouted at him in Russian. Without hesitating, Black shot the man twice, killing him.

The gunfire attracted the attention of the two guards in the lab as they raced toward the door. Black sprinted around the corner and crouched low, waiting for them to emerge. As they did, he took them each out with a couple shots.

Then everything fell eerily quiet.

Black eased inside the lab door, where he was met by wide eyes and slack-jawed faces.

"Dr. Matthews?" Black asked as he scanned the room.

One man raised his hand and stepped forward. "You're not going to hurt me, are you?"

Black shook his head. "No, I'm here to get you out."

"My invention didn't kill anyone, did it?" Matthews asked.

"Your invention?"

"Night-Night, the ultrasonic device I built for that monster who's kept me and all these other people here for the past couple of years."

Black nodded. "There's one person who's dead because of it—Antoine. Now, if anyone wants out of here, you need to come with me."

"And we need to hurry," one of the scientists said. "Vladi will be back any time now."

"Vladi?" Black asked.

The man nodded. "Yes, he's the one who runs this place, and he always has at least two of this thugs with him."

"All right," Black said. "Let's go."

All the other researchers raced toward the door, except Matthews.

"There's something I need to do first," he said, hustling over toward a supply closet. He started grabbing bottles and putting them on the table.

"What are you doing?" Black asked. "We need to go."

"Acetone," Matthews said, showing the label to Black. "I don't want anyone getting their hands on this research."

"And what's this going to do?"

"It's going to help burn this place to the ground, something that should've happened a long time ago."

Black helped Matthews douse the liquid all over the lab, while the other workers waited in the hallway.

"Hurry up, Aaron," one of the women called. "We need to go."

When they were finished, a faint smile spread around the corner of Matthews's lips. "This has been a long time coming."

He pulled a zippo lighter out and tossed it into the room. Immediately, flames engulfed the entire area.

"Go, go, go!" Matthews said, urging everyone up the stairs.

Black was just about to join them when he heard a deep booming voice.

"What do you think you're doing?" Vladi bellowed.

Black poked his head around the corner to see a muscular bald man crinkling his nose as he stuck it in the air.

"What's that smell?" Vladi demanded.

"Plug your ears," Black said in a hushed tone. Then he activated the device he'd lifted off Antoine's dead body. It only took a few seconds before Valdi and his two men were lying on the ground in a heap.

After navigating around the bodies, Black led the hostages outside and through the pedestrian gate where Shields was waiting on the other side with a van.

Everyone hustled inside without saying a word.

Once they were situated, Matthews grabbed Black by the shoulder. "I was trying to destroy that technology. If that falls into the wrong hands—"

"Then make sure it doesn't," Black said as he offered the mechanism to Matthews.

He took it and studied it before stuffing it into his pocket. Matthews smiled for the first time since Black had laid eyes on the scientist.

"Aren't you going to ask how we found you?" Black asked.

Matthews shook his head. "I don't need to ask. I already know."

"You make sure you give your daughter a big hug when we arrive back home," Shields said. "If it weren't for her, we never would've gone looking for you again."

"That doesn't surprise me," Matthews said. "She's relentless."

Black leaned back in his seat and listened to the escapees share stories of survival as they expressed their relief over finally breaking out of what had become a virtual prison for them.

This is why I do what I do.

CHAPTER 38

Two days later
Washington, D.C.

BLACK SIFTED THROUGH the reports on the conference room table with Shields, reviewing everything that had been written about the mission. The redactions barely made the documents readable, but they were necessary to satisfy the terms of Firestorm's existence. When major operations on foreign soil were completed, a record of the group's activities was required to protect them from scurrilous accusations, just like the ones the late Senator Wilson Wellington hurled at them.

"Everything look good to you?" Blunt asked as he entered the room.

Black slapped the table and nodded. "It looks perfect."

"Shields?" Blunt asked.

"Looks good to me, sir," she said.

"In that case, we can consider this mission

successfully closed."

"Finally," Black said. "Were you there when Dr. Matthews was reunited with his daughter?"

"That was an amazing moment," Blunt said. "Made the past week worth it. I'm sorry you didn't get to experience it with me."

"It's the job," Black said. "Nobody is supposed to know we exist. In fact, nobody is even supposed to know I'm alive."

"You did a good job of staying under the radar," Blunt said. "I did have to do a little work with Besserman to make sure that your face was deleted from some closed-circuit footage when you weren't in disguise. But your secret is still safe."

Black stacked the papers up and shoved them toward Blunt. "Speaking of Besserman, were you able to figure out anything regarding what happened with my father? Was Wellington telling the truth about there being something else?"

"We're still digging, but apparently there were some other personnel files of his that were actually destroyed," Blunt said. "Besserman asked Mallory Kauffman to look into the disappearance of some other records that your father was indexed as mentioned in. However, they're all gone. But we'll keep looking. Something will pop up soon enough. Whoever was ultimately responsible for your father's death will have to answer for what they did."

Black sighed. "Okay, thanks for all you're doing. I just want justice for my dad."

"Me, too."

They concluded their meeting by discussing their next mission involving a commander who'd disappeared off the grid. Once they deconvened, Shields followed Blunt into the hall.

"Want to go get a drink after work, maybe catch a game?" she suggested.

"How about something a little more low key?" Black asked. "I wouldn't mind the company, but I'm not keen on the idea of going back out in public again if I can help it."

"Your place this evening then?"

"Sounds great."

Black finished up the rest of his day and then drove home. He thought about his father and the final excruciating moments of his life. While Black was sure there were more painful ways to die, getting dragged to death behind a truck driven by Taliban soldiers had to rank up there as one of the most humiliating.

Feeling sentimental, Black retrieved a box of his father's belongings and was digging through it when Shields knocked at the door. She came in carrying a six-pack of Black's favorite IPA beer along with a bottle of wine.

"This ought to help us take the edge off," she said as she made a bee line for the kitchen.

"After the past couple of weeks we've had, we need it."

Shields poured herself a glass of Merlot and then cracked open a bottle for Black before handing it to him. She glanced down at the articles and items strewn across the coffee table.

"What's all this?" she asked.

"I just got to thinking about my dad and how I wished I would've gotten to know him better," Black said. "Or know him at all, really. What happened to him almost feels like someone else's story sometime, and I just wanted to reconnect with him a bit. And this is the only way for me to do it since my mom is gone too."

Shields sat on the couch and picked up a photo from Captain Black's squadron. She studied the image closely and pointed out Wilson Wellington standing near the back.

"There's the murderer," she said. "Seeing this image after knowing all we know is somewhat surreal."

Black sighed. "But what do we really know? That everything we've been told up to this point may not even be true? It's frustrating to no end."

Black waved his hand dismissively, brushing up against the side of the box. It tipped over, the contents spilling out across the floor.

A gold medal with a red, white, and blue ribbon clanked onto the floor. Shields scooped up the prize and handed it to Black.

"What did he win this for?" she asked as she gave the object to him.

He cocked his head to one side and inspected the inscription on the front for a moment. "To be honest, I have no idea."

As he went to place the medal back into the box, he shook it. Something rattled around inside.

"What's this?" he asked aloud.

He fiddled with the back, which appeared to open somehow. After a few seconds of turning and twisting and pushing and pulling, the back popped off. Inside was a small piece of paper folded up several times. Black unraveled the note and read it aloud.

"Call Myron Tillman," Black said before mumbling the number to himself.

"Who's that?" Shields asked.

"Beats me," Black said.

Then he flipped over the note. On the back, the words "Blue Moon Rising" was scribbled in pen.

"This guy has the answers you're looking for?" Shields asked.

Black shrugged. "There's only one way to find out."

He wanted to dial the number right away. Refusing to wait, he punched the number into his phone. After several rings, a pre-recorded message from the telephone company stated that the number Black had dialed was no longer in service.

"If you feel you've reached this number in error . . ."

"Now what?" Shields asked. "Want me to start digging into who this guy was and see if we can track him down today?"

"Only if you want to," Black said.

"You know I love a good mystery."

"Of course, it may turn out to be nothing," Black reminded her.

"We'll find out soon enough," she said, grabbing the note. "I'll get to it in the morning."

"I'd appreciate that," Black said.

An hour later, Shields decided to go home. Black didn't mind as he wanted to return to memory lane. But that was an exercise that didn't last long. He'd answered some questions, but he'd raised more in the process. Many, many more.

Black called Blunt to thank him for all his help in rescuing Dr. Matthews from Estonia.

"I think we take your depth of knowledge for granted," Black said.

"It's called being old and connected," Blunt said. "It's nothing special."

"I beg to differ," Black said.

"Is that all you wanted to tell me?" Blunt asked. "I'm guessing there's another reason you called."

"It's about my dad. I found a number hidden on a piece of paper tucked away in one of his medals tonight. I don't know if it means anything or not, but it had the guy's name along with the name Blue Moon Rising on the back."

"That must've been what your father stumbled onto," Blunt said.

"Are you sure everything's above board with what you're doing?"

"Positive," Blunt said. "We'll get this figured out."

"No," Black said. "Let me figure it out. If I find out something you should know about, I'll tell you. I don't want you to put yourself in danger with the organization in case there's something to it."

"All right," Blunt said. "I'll give you that courtesy. But the second you think something questionable is going on, you better let me know."

"Will do," Black said. "And thanks again."

"Of course," Blunt said. "But make sure you get rested up. We've got a new assignment that just came in this evening."

"I'll be ready," Black said before he hung up the phone.

And he would be.

THE END

ACKNOWLEDGMENTS

I am grateful to so many people who have helped with the creation of this project and the entire Titus Black series.

Krystal Wade was a big help in editing this book as always.

I would also like to thank my advance reader team for all their input in improving this book along with all the other readers who have enthusiastically embraced the story of Titus Black. Stay tuned ... there's more Titus Black coming soon.

ABOUT THE AUTHOR

R.J. PATTERSON is an award-winning writer living in southeastern Idaho. He first began his illustrious writing career as a sports journalist, recording his exploits on the soccer fields in England as a young boy. Then when his father told him that people would pay him to watch sports if he would write about what he saw, he went all in. He landed his first writing job at age 15 as a sports writer for a daily newspaper in Orangeburg, S.C. He later attended earned a degree in newspaper journalism from the University of Georgia, where he took a job covering high school sports for the award-winning *Athens Banner-Herald* and *Daily News*.

He later became the sports editor of *The Valdosta Daily Times* before working in the magazine world as an editor and freelance journalist. He has won numerous writing awards, including a national award for his investigative reporting on a sordid tale surrounding an NCAA investigation over the University of Georgia football program.

R.J. enjoys the great outdoors of the Northwest while living there with his wife and four children. He still follows sports closely. He also loves connecting with readers and would love to hear from you. To stay updated about future projects, connect with him over Facebook or on the interwebs at www.RJPbooks.com and sign up for his newsletter.